"All right, here's the plan,"

Patrick announced. "I put your shelving together. You spend Saturday in the park with my nieces and me."

Brooke never blinked an eye. "You've got a deal."

"Not so fast," he said, holding up a hand to caution her. "This looks like a lot of work, and since you're partly to blame for my having to cater to the twins on Saturday, there's one more condition to this little bargain."

"Oh? And what's that?" She looked so suspicious, Patrick wondered if she could read minds.

"I get a kiss for every shelf I put together."

Instead of slapping his face, the response he expected to his impulsive, outrageous, totally bizarre suggestion, Brooke actually seemed to consider it quite seriously.

"Each shelf or each unit?" she asked.

"Each shelf." Crazy, Patrick might be, but never a fool.

"That's—" she paused to figure; her eyes rounded "—eighty kisses!"

Patrick nodded. "And five are payable in advance."

Dear Reader,

June . . . a month of courtship and romance, white lace and wedding vows. And at Silhouette Romance we're celebrating those June brides and grooms with some very special tales of love and marriage. Best of all—YOU'RE INVITED!

As every bride knows, you can't march down the aisle without the essentials, starting with *Something Old*—a fun-filled look at love with an older man—from Toni Collins. Gabriella Thorne falls for her boss, Adrian Lacross—a handsome and oh-so-charming . . . vampire. Can the love of a good woman change Adrian's fly-by-night romantic ways?

Something New was in store for prim-and-proper Eve Winthrop the day the new high school principal came to town. Carla Cassidy brings us the *irresistible* Brice Maxwell, who shakes up a sleepy Oklahoma town and dares Eve to take a walk on the wild side.

Linda Varner brings us *Something Borrowed* from the magical land of Oz! A tornado whisked Brooke Brady into Patrick Sawyer's life. Is handsome Patrick really a heartless Tin Man—or Brooke's very own heart's desire?

Something Blue is an unexpected little package from the stork for newly divorced Teddy Falco and Quinn Barnett. Jayne Addison's heartwarming style lends special magic to this story of a couple reunited by the miracle of their new baby.

Elizabeth August gives the final touch to our wedding bouquet with *Lucky Penny*. Celina Warley and Reid Prescott weren't looking for a marriage with love, but with luck, would love find them?

Our FABULOUS FATHERS series continues with an unforgettable hero and dad—Judd Tanner, in *One Man's Vow* by Diana Whitney. Judd is a devoted father who will go the limit to protect his four children—even if it means missing out on the love of one very special woman.

In the months to come look for books by more of your favorite authors—Annette Broadrick, Diana Palmer, Lucy Gordon, Suzanne Carey and many more.

Until then, happy reading!

Anne Canadeo
Senior Editor

SOMETHING BORROWED
Linda Varner

Silhouette
R O M A N C E™
Published by Silhouette Books New York
America's Publisher of Contemporary Romance

SILHOUETTE BOOKS
300 East 42nd St., New York, N.Y. 10017

SOMETHING BORROWED

Copyright © 1993 by Linda Varner Palmer

ISBN: 0-373-08943-0

First Silhouette Books printing June 1993

All the characters in this book have no existence outside the imagination of the author and have no relation whatsoever to anyone bearing the same name or names. They are not even distantly inspired by any individual known or unknown to the author, and all incidents are pure invention.

®: Trademark used under license and registered in the United States Patent and Trademark Office and in other countries.

Printed in the U.S.A.

LINDA VARNER

admits that her own romance was nothing like that of her characters in *Something Borrowed*. "Oh, it was love at first sight, all right," she says fondly. "But Jim and I were only in ninth grade when we fell, so a whirlwind courtship was definitely out of the question!" Today, she remains happily married to her junior high school sweetheart, and they live in their Arkansas hometown with their two children.

Patrick Sawyer on marriage:

Marriage? It's okay, I guess. I mean, I do have this big ol' house and no one to share it with. But I haven't had much luck with love, so it would take a mighty special woman to make me throw caution to the wind and give it a whirl.

Brooke Brady on marriage:

Of course I believe in marriage. I've had every detail of my wedding planned—from gown to groom—since I was five. Too bad life is no fairy tale. I really had my heart set on a handsome prince....

Prologue

"Tu-Tu," Brooke Brady said to the stuffed poodle sitting in the passenger seat of her car. "Something tells me we're not in Oregon anymore."

The fluffy white poodle, whose sagging midriff sported a pink net ruffle, said nothing, of course, and Brooke laughed aloud, glad no one was along to hear her foolishness.

Not that she hadn't wished for company every now and then during this little move. She had. But for the most part, the three-day trip had been a perfect blend of solitude, adventure and luck.

She'd especially enjoyed the changing scenery along the way, ranging from the purple mountains of her native northwest United States to this Texas horizon, so flat she could see miles of highway, grass and open sky.

Brooke scanned that open sky and hoped the rainstorm threatening her this past hour would hold off a little longer. She wasn't completely sure the old rental trailer hooked to the back of her car—the one that held everything she treasured in this world—wouldn't leak.

On that thought, Brooke frowned and glanced back at that same trailer. Her frown vanished almost immediately, and she bubbled with laughter again, imagining the sight she must make rolling down this Texas freeway: sleek red convertible with the top up, battered gray trailer bouncing along behind.

But Brooke didn't worry long how she looked. She had more important things on her mind, most urgent among them locating a good motel once she reached Amarillo, now only five miles away.

Five measly miles.

Yesss! Brooke heaved a heartfelt sigh, her thoughts on what lay ahead—new job, new life—and then on what lay behind—old friends.

Scary business, this pulling up roots, this starting over. But a woman did what she had to do, and Brooke Brady had to find herself a home.

She just had to. . . .

And Texas was as good a place as any to do it.

Suddenly loud thunder crashed into Brooke's musings. She started violently, then inspected the solid wall of clouds to the southwest, not for the first time marveling at their color. A weird sort of greenish brown, they hung suspended just above the golden horizon and in sharp contrast to it.

Brooke frowned thoughtfully, then reached out and flipped on her radio. Since it was tuned to her favorite Portland station, static blared forth, but in seconds that was replaced by the beat of a country ballad when she found a local station.

She let the sound wash over her and relaxed... until a disc jockey stopped the music to announce a tornado warning. It seemed that a funnel cloud had been sighted by state troopers just southwest of Amarillo and anyone in the area should be prepared to take cover if necessary.

"Oh, no," Brooke breathed in dismay.

She'd long ago wondered about the absence of Friday afternoon traffic this close to the city. Now she guessed it was because the natives were hiding indoors.

Brooke gulped and anxiously studied the horizon again. This time she discerned the definite motion of some of the clouds. Were they spinning?

She couldn't really tell since the sky grew darker by the minute. It could easily have been seven o'clock instead of five-thirty on this May evening.

Brooke shivered, wishing she were already settled in some motel. She did not like this kind of weather— never had—a fact she blamed on getting caught up in a tree during an electrical storm at the tender age of five.

If she lived to be one hundred, she would not forget the wind that had tried to shake her from the branches, the lightning that stabbed the ground, or the rolling thunder.

Lord, what a sound.

At once as nervous now as then, Brooke sucked in a couple of deep breaths. That calming tactic actually seemed to work until she gave in to the temptation to peruse the heavens again.

This time she saw what looked to be—could it be?— one of those funnel clouds she'd just heard about on the radio.

Her overactive imagination?

Maybe.

Brooke had never seen a funnel cloud except on television and didn't really know what one looked like. Nonetheless, the whisper swirl of gray-white now hovering high above the terrain was definitely cone-shaped and had begun to dip ominously toward the ground.

Brooke hit the brake, never taking her eyes off the mesmerizing sight, still miles away at this point, but headed right toward her as far as she could tell. The deejay had said to take cover. What kind? she frantically wondered even as she spied an overpass a quarter of a mile ahead.

There were many such bridges, built, she'd been told, to accommodate the farmers whose vast fields were necessarily crisscrossed by freeways. Constructed of concrete, they were surely solid and would provide excellent protection.

But was she really in danger...or overreacting?

Another glance at the suspicious cloud, now three times as large and almost touching ground, assured her that she was not overreacting. A second weather advisory cinched it, and without further hesitation, Brook stomped the accelerator.

Her eye ever on the sky, she sped to the overpass, which turned out to be frighteningly farther away than she'd first thought. Brooke's heart thumped with fear by the time she braked, grabbed her purse and leaped from her car.

But instead of dashing for cover, she stood rooted to the highway, hypnotized by the unleashed might, the sheer raw power of the storm.

The roar of the wind deafened her. Tree limbs...pieces of tin...all sorts of debris swept across the road and hung up in the barbed-wire fences bordering every field. Rain and then hail began to pelt the ground and her head.

Brooke screamed and dashed for cover. Staggering against the force of the gale, she stumbled and struggled up the sharp incline of the embankment, crawling the last few feet to the ledge formed where the embankment met the underside of the overpass. There she huddled, sobbing, while all hell broke loose around her.

Wind buffeted Brooke's body, plucked at her clothes and stole her breath. Time stood still—or seemed to—leaving her stranded in her nightmare.

And through it all, Brooke anchored her gaze to her car—scarlet reality in a whirling phantasmagoria.

That reality rocked, tipped, flipped over and spun.

Then right before her eyes, it vanished—along with the trailer—swallowed up whole by a Texas twister.

Chapter One

Patrick Sawyer loved storms—always had. As a child, he'd run outside at the first sprinkle of rain and stayed there, usually on the front porch swing, until the last rumble of thunder died away. As an adult, he put his penchant to good use by volunteering to help the Texas Weather Service watch for tornadoes when conditions threatened.

He'd trained intensively for this job of "spotter" and loved being involved. For that very reason he now sat in perfect contentment behind the steering wheel of his pickup truck, which he'd parked on a bridge near Emerald City, a suburb of Amarillo.

A steady stream of weather reports squawked from his emergency radio. An unseasonably coolish breeze blew in through the open window, bringing with it the pungent smell of rain. Lightning snaked ominously across the southwest sky, silver bright against black-dark clouds.

Patrick heard a low growl of thunder and was amazed when his skin crawled in response. No false alarm, this call, he suddenly realized, his senses automatically quickening.

"Debris! Debris! We have a tornado! Repeat. *We have a touchdown!*"

The words blared from the radio, almost drowned by ear-splitting static. Patrick tensed and anxiously scanned the sky for any sign of a twister while the obviously agitated spotter repeated his warning, then gave his exact location.

"Attention, all units," interjected another voice, this one calmer and closer. "Unit Eight reports a touchdown five miles west of Amarillo off I-40. Unit Six, can you verify?"

"Affirmative," came the reply, another static-filled transmission. "On the ground and headed northeast for Emerald City."

Emerald City?

Patrick sat bolt upright and looked down over the little community he loved. So named because of its lush lawns and evergreen trees, the area had been home to Patrick for some six years. He had friends and family here, not to mention a Laundromat, a dairy bar, and a brand new car wash.

Patrick could see that very car wash from his vantage point atop the bridge, and only minutes ago he'd been working there, preparing for tomorrow's grand opening. Then the call to duty had come. . . .

Patrick swallowed the lump of fear in his throat. At that moment the earsplitting wail of a siren warned the good citizens of Emerald City to take cover. Patrick, his gaze once more on the rolling southwest sky, started the engine of his truck, fully prepared to make a dash of his own for safety, if need be. Since it now began to sprinkle rain, he rolled up the window, too.

"Unit Ten, do you see a funnel cloud?" It was the dispatcher again.

"Negative," replied a fellow spotter, one of Patrick's neighbors.

"Unit Twelve?"

Patrick picked up the microphone and pressed a button. "I see the cloud headed this way, but no touchdown. Repeating . . . no touchdown."

And there wasn't, thank God. From all appearances, the funnel cloud had ascended, as they sometimes did, and with luck would pass over Emerald City with minimal damage.

A violent gust of wind suddenly rocked the truck and whistled shrilly around the windows. Raindrops splashed onto the windshield, increasing in intensity until he turned on the wipers so he could see.

Patrick, the connoisseur of tempests, actually felt a shiver of fear at that moment, but did not abandon his post even when hail began to pelt his vehicle, raising a hellish din. Instead he turned up the volume on the radio.

That was when he heard the roar—that unmistakable roar that sounded, according to thousands of witnesses through the years, like a freight train.

A tornado for sure. But not on the ground.

High overhead it vented its fury. And high overhead it passed through Emerald City, doing no more damage than dumping a lakeload of rain and hail, lifting loose shingles, uprooting trees....

And dropping a bright red convertible smack on Patrick Sawyer's car wash.

He blinked to clear his vision when it fell from the sky, then scrambled right out of the truck to stand out in the elements so he could see better.

No, he quickly confirmed. His eyes had not played tricks on him. A car had dropped out of the sky and landed on his car wash—the car wash he'd worked so hard to build, the car wash he'd planned to open for business *tomorrow*.

"Unit Twelve. Unit Twelve. Do you have a report yet?"

Patrick sprang to life, reaching a thoroughly rain-soaked arm inside the truck to snatch up the microphone.

"No touchdown. Just rain, hail and high winds."

"Any damage?"

"Minimal from my vantage point, except—" he gulped "—there's now a red car on top of my car wash."

"Noted. Unit Twenty, do you have a report?"

And so life—and the twister—went on. His duty done, Patrick slipped back behind the steering wheel and sped on across the bridge into town. The moment he reached the car wash, he killed the engine and leaped out to run over to it, oblivious to the rain that still sprinkled down on his head.

"Unbelievable," he muttered as he walked around what once must have been one gorgeous sports car. Almost invisible in a twist of chrome bumper, he spotted an Oregon license plate and briefly wondered just how long that roadster had flown the not-so-friendly skies of Texas.

And what about passengers . . . ?

At that instant another car wheeled up—this one white with the insignia of the Texas State Troopers on its door. Out jumped the most beautiful woman Patrick had ever seen, clutching a straw purse as though everything she owned was in it. Petite, blonde, well-built and clearly distraught, she ran right over to that red car and burst into tears.

"Look at it! Just look at it!" she raved between sobs as she paced back and forth in front of the remains of her vehicle. "What a mess." She waved the purse; she stomped a sandaled foot; she brushed her long wet hair out of her face with agitated swipes. Patrick's heart went out to her instantly.

Whose wouldn't?

But to his amazement, another body part responded with equal enthusiasm. That shocking, totally inappropriate reaction caught him off guard and irritated the hell out of him.

"And where's my trailer?" the woman in question next wailed, turning on him as though he knew the answer and wouldn't tell it.

"Don't look at me!" Patrick heard himself snap at her, words he regretted almost instantly.

Venting his anger with himself—and misdirecting it to her—wasn't going to help their situation. And it certainly wasn't her fault the tornado had dropped her vehicle on his car wash, although, if her outraged expression was any clue, she thought he believed it was.

"Just where do you get off talking to me like that?" she demanded, whirling on him, huge hazel eyes flashing.

Patrick took a step back from her fury—fury he probably deserved. He opened his mouth, fully intending to apologize...until his gaze touched her full, pouty lips. He gulped and quickly dropped that gaze...right down to her breasts, perfectly shaped, plastered in wet T-shirt and heaving with agitation.

Holy...

Further inspection of her person revealed a tiny waist and golden-tanned legs any model would envy. Patrick's hormones—even the ones that had been peacefully snoozing for the past two years—went totally berserk. The mutiny left him weak-kneed, trembling and a little bit crazy.

"Did you hear me?"

"Hell, yeah, I heard you!" he retorted in utter self-disgust. "And I—"

The screech of brakes—an unmistakably familiar sound Patrick had heard many times and kept forgetting to do anything about—saved him from making a bigger fool of himself. He turned expectantly toward the sound and was not surprised when his mother sprang from her brother's minivan.

"I heard the report on the radio!" Sarah Sawyer exclaimed as she hurried over to them. Quickly she inspected the car and then the young blonde, in turn. Something of the young woman's distress must have transmitted to Patrick's mother. "Your car?"

"Y-yes." Her lower lip trembled.

"Oh, my dear—"

More squealing brakes... these also familiar, Patrick realized when he turned and spied his sister, Cynthia Kimbrell, hopping out of his mother's vehicle, a four-door sedan. The back door also flew open, and from it spilled his twin nieces, Emmaline and Michele. They ran right up to him as fast as their five-year-old legs could carry them.

"You were on the radio," Emmy exclaimed, blue eyes dancing with excitement.

"Is this the car?" Shelly added, as though tornadoes airlifted autos every day.

"Hush, girls," Cynthia cautioned, her eyes on her mother, now hugging the blonde. "Hers?" she whispered to Patrick.

He nodded.

"Poor thing."

Yeah, he silently agreed, thoroughly ashamed of his display of temper mere moments ago. She certainly had her problems. But then, so did he....

Thank goodness he'd mailed back those insurance papers.

On that thought, Patrick tensed. He *had* mailed them back, hadn't he? Frantically he searched through his memory for the act of dropping that long white envelope into the mailbox.

"Everyone okay here?" It was the state trooper, Sam Richardson, whom Patrick had known for years, just now climbing out of his car to join them. Patrick looked over at him and was surprised to find that several citizens of Emerald City had appeared from nowhere and now stood all around marveling at the sight of an automobile perched atop the remains of the community's newest car wash.

"We're all okay," Sarah Sawyer said in response to the trooper's question. "I'm not sure about this young woman, though. What's your name, dear?"

"Brooke Brady," the blonde replied, easing free of Sarah's embrace, her voice shaky with distress.

"Where are you from?"

"Portland, Oregon."

"Where are you headed?"

"Amarillo. I have a new job there."

"So you're moving?"

Again Brooke nodded. She glanced toward her car and winced. "I was towing a trailer. All my things are ... in ... it...." Her voice trailed off to nothingness. The color drained from her face. Her shoulders sagged.

Instinctively, Patrick leaped forward and, just as her knees buckled, grabbed her. So valiant was his effort to break her fall that he stumbled to one knee on the concrete. But she didn't hit the ground or her head, and that made pain worthwhile.

"Brooke? Brooke Brady?"

Gradually, Brooke became aware of a woman's voice, calling to her in the dark. She deliberately ignored the sound...until a cool cloth was pressed to her face, clearing the confusion, bringing harsh reality and painful memories.

Brooke opened her eyes and found herself flat on her back on something—a blanket?—surrounded by strange faces. She recognized one of them: a brunette woman with the kindest smile in the world. She also recognized another: a man. A long, tall Texan with dark hair, cowboy boots and no manners at all.

"Thank goodness," breathed the woman. "Are you okay, dear?"

Brooke nodded, and struggled to sit. Several of the dozen or so people hovering over her helped, and in moments she was able to stand on legs downright shaky.

"I fainted?" She'd never done that before and couldn't believe she had now.

"Yes, and no wonder. Is there someone I can call to come get you? Friends? Family, maybe?"

"I have no one," Brooke said, a truth that filled her eyes with fresh tears. Impatiently she blinked them back. "But I'll be all right...just as soon as I get to the city." She scanned the crowd for the state trooper who'd rescued her an eternity ago—the one on whose radio they'd heard the report that a red car had dropped out of the sky in—what was it?—Emerald City? Brooke felt certain he would give her a ride on in to Amarillo.

He was nowhere to be seen.

The woman, clearly picking up on her confusion, lay a comforting arm across her shoulder. "What is it, dear?"

"I was looking for the trooper. I thought he could give me a lift to—"

"He got an emergency call and left. Patrick, here, will be glad to take you into the city...but not now. You're coming home with us tonight. Tomorrow, when you feel better, you can go to Amarillo."

"But—"

"No buts." Brooke found herself propelled toward an electric-blue minivan with handicap license plates. "This is a mother speaking. Maybe not yours, but a mother all the same. I can see that you're dead on your feet. You need a hot bath, a good meal and some sleep. I intend to see that you get them."

"But—"

"Come along now." The woman's tone brooked no argument, which was just as well. For the minute Brooke stepped in the direction of the van, her tragedy hit her square in the knees, which threatened to buckle again and caused her to stumble.

"Patrick," the woman quietly ordered, even as the man with no manners swept her up in strong arms and covered the distance to the vehicle. Without a word, he deposited her into it and fastened the seat belt.

Their gazes locked for just a second, but that was long enough for Brooke to see a flash of something— what?—in his dark eyes. Every hormone in her body leaped to attention in response, leaving her bewildered and disgusted.

Good grief! This Patrick guy was a total jerk. Obviously she did need a good night's sleep.

The door on the driver's side opened and the dark-haired woman slipped in behind the steering wheel.

"We'll have you in dry clothes in no time, Brooke," she said as she started the engine.

"You know my name," Brooke replied, mustering up a smile. "But I don't know yours."

"Sarah Sawyer," her companion offered, smiling back. "I'm Patrick's mother."

"Oh." Something of Brooke's opinion of Patrick must have shown on her face or revealed itself in her voice. At any rate, Sarah turned to her in some surprise.

"You don't like my son?"

"Well..." Brooke didn't want to hurt the woman's feelings. "He was rather rude to me."

Sarah's jaw dropped. "The rather intense young man wearing the striped cowboy shirt and the snakeskin boots?"

Brooke nodded rather hesitantly.

"He was rude to you?"

She nodded again.

Sarah, clearly astounded, said nothing for a moment. "Then I must apologize for him. He isn't usually rude to beautiful young women. He's never rude to *anyone,* in fact.'' She shook her head slowly from side to side and said nothing more until she turned the van onto a street named Baumgartner and then into a driveway. ''This is it.''

Brooke looked between the raindrops sprinkled over the windshield and peered at the house. Sarah braked the vehicle under tall oak trees, killed the engine, and smiled at her.

''There's no place like home,'' she said with utter sincerity.

Brooke could only agree. Heaven knew she'd give anything for one of her own this minute.

''Come on in. The sooner you get yourself a hot bath, the better you'll feel. I'll find something of Cynthia's for you to put on.''

''Cynthia?'' Brooke repeated as she climbed out of the van and followed Sarah up the walk of the three-story gingerbread-style house.

''My daughter. Did you notice the redhead with the twin girls back there at Patrick's car wash?''

Brooke did—vaguely—and so nodded.

''That was my daughter, Cynthia. Her husband is in the military—active duty in Alaska until June. She and her two girls are living here with the rest of us.''

''The rest of you?''

Sarah laughed. ''Never mind. You'll meet them all later . . . well, all but my son, Randy. He's in Nashville this week.''

Brooke nodded rather dazedly, then frowned when something Sarah said belatedly registered in her brain.

''That car wash belonged to your son?''

"Yes." She sighed. "He was planning to open it for business tomorrow."

"You mean it's *new?*"

"Mmm-hmm."

"Oh, dear. No wonder he was angry with me."

"I'm sure he wasn't angry with you. After all, it wasn't your fault the tornado dropped your car just there."

Tell him that, Brooke silently retorted. Aloud she said nothing, however, instead turning her attention to the quaint wooden structure before them. It looked as though it belonged in a fairy tale...the same one in which Brooke found herself stranded.

For the third time her precarious situation hit home. But this time she didn't stumble. How could she with Sarah Sawyer's arm around her waist, firmly guiding her up the stairs?

Brooke took comfort in that warm support, for just a moment reminded of the mother she'd lost to cancer so many years ago. Things would've been different if that mother had lived.

Indeed, this whole Texas adventure would never have happened.

But it had happened, and she would have to deal with it. Brooke just hoped she could find the energy. Thank goodness for Sarah Sawyer's generous offer to share her home. A night in this warm atmosphere could only boost Brooke's flagging spirits.

At that moment a sedan and then a truck wheeled into the drive. Brooke paused on the porch before entering the door Sarah had opened for her. Turning, she saw Cynthia and the two girls get out of the car. Then she saw Patrick get out of the truck.

What's he doing here? she wondered, the next second giving herself a mental scolding. The house belonged to his mother, after all. Who was Brooke Brady, a woman at the mercy of strangers, to tell the man he couldn't come home for a hopefully short visit?

On that thought, Brooke squared her shoulders, smiled at her hostess and stepped into the foyer. She glanced around, noting tasteful carpeting and wallpaper, beautiful antique furnishings, and a winding staircase.

"You have a lovely home, Sarah," Brooke said.

"Oh, it isn't mine, dear," the woman responded with an airy wave of her hand. "It's Patrick's. I'm a guest here . . . just like you."

Chapter Two

Stunned to her toes, Brooke couldn't begin to reply to that. And it wasn't necessary since Cynthia joined them in the foyer at just that moment. Sarah asked her daughter to take care of introductions, then excused herself to the kitchen to check on the meal in her slow-cooker.

Moments later Patrick burst into the house, a squirming, squealing child tucked under each arm. Apparently he'd just scooped them up, since they both still protested the manhandling.

"You're wet!"

"Yuck!"

Their wiggling made it clear they wanted down, and Patrick instantly obliged by setting both on their feet. He didn't release either until they gave him a kiss, however, a scene that would have warmed Brooke's heart under normal circumstances.

Unfortunately these were not normal circumstances. She did not care for this good-looking Texan with his short temper...whether or not he was excellent with children.

Laughing at her girls, Cynthia turned to Brooke. "Hi. My name is Cynthia Kimbrell. These two munchkins are my daughters, Emmaline and Michele, otherwise known as Emmy and Shelly."

Brooke barely heard, so fascinated was she by how very alike the two girls looked. Identically upturned noses. Strawberry-blond eyebrows and lashes. A generous sprinkling of freckles. Brooke also noted that Emmy wore a blue bow in her hair while Shelly wore a green one. Was that how to tell them apart? she wondered.

"And you've already met my brother, Patrick Sawyer," Cynthia continued.

"Sort of." Brooke managed a smile for the pretty redhead that faded just a little when she politely included the man in question. "I understand this is your house," she said to him, "and I really don't want to misput you further. Couldn't you just take me to a motel or something?"

"There's no motel in Emerald City," he solemnly informed her. "And you won't misput me if you stay here. We have plenty of room."

"How are you feeling?" Cynthia then asked Brooke.

"Oh, I'm all right."

"No, you're not and won't be until you get into some dry clothes," Sarah sternly interjected from where she stood in the doorway. "Now I want you to take a hot bath right away. You're blue with cold." She glanced at Patrick. "A change of clothing might not be a bad idea for you, either, son. As for you—" she looked at Cynthia "—please set the table for dinner. I want to see after Brooke myself."

"Yes, ma'am," Patrick replied, words that slipped off his tongue so easily Brooke grinned in spite of herself. Cynthia's quick echo of his reply only broadened her grin and told her who ruled the roost around here.

Brooke wondered briefly what had happened to their father, then lost that thought when Sarah put a hand to the small of her back and propelled her toward the stairs.

"Come with me. We'll find you something to wear, and while you're bathing, I'll get Randy's room ready for you. It's up on the third floor."

Randy? "I—I really need to call my insurance company about my car before I do anything."

"Thirty minutes won't make a bit of difference to your car," stated Sarah, hustling Brooke ever onward and upward. "But it just might to your health. Bath first."

"Yes, ma'am," Brooke heard herself say as she climbed dutifully up the stairs, which creaked wonderfully with every step. When they reached the second floor, Sarah pointed out the bathroom, then led the way to a bedroom just down the hall. She walked so fast, Brooke managed only a passing glance at her surroundings. One impression surfaced: simple elegance.

The room that belonged to Cynthia confirmed it. Massive enough to hold a double bed, a dresser, two bureaus, a love seat and a rocker, the area's papered walls, floor-to-ceiling windows and lacy curtains bespoke another age.

Brooke loved it and opened her mouth to tell Sarah, but the woman had her head buried in a closet. Finally she turned and thrust a red shirt and a pair of jeans at Brooke. Then she walked over to the bureau and began to sort through the contents of one of the drawers.

"Have all of you always lived together in this house?" Brooke asked, wondering how Patrick came to be the owner of what appeared to be a family home.

"Oh, no. I had a place of my own until about a year ago. The neighborhood became so rundown that Patrick insisted I move in with him. Shortly after, he gathered up Cynthia and the girls. Next, he talked my younger son, Randy, into joining us. Then Gilbert."

Good grief! "Gilbert?"

Sarah, a nylon gown and chenille robe thrown over one arm, turned to smile at Brooke. "Gilbert Mercer, my brother. He's a painter."

"No kidding. Oils or acrylics?"

Sarah laughed. "Houses, actually. He had an accident six months ago that put him in a wheelchair—quite a blow to a man so physical. He lost all heart, refused to do his therapy. Anyway, Patrick built a wheelchair ramp, remodeled a little inside, and insisted that Gil move in so I could help him rehabilitate. I'm good at that sort of thing."

So much for Sarah ruling the roost, Brooke realized. From all appearances, Patrick controlled this flock, at least as far as the big decisions were concerned. In fact, he sounded more like the man of the house than the eldest son, and in spite of what he'd said about having plenty of room, he probably didn't appreciate his mother inviting strangers to stay overnight.

"This is so embarrassing," Brooke murmured at that thought.

"What is?"

"My staying here. I really shouldn't, you know."

"Why ever not?"

"Because I'm intruding."

"Nonsense. We're glad to help out. Don't cheat us of the pleasure."

"Some pleasure. I doubt that Randy will appreciate being rooted from his room."

"But he isn't here," Sarah replied. "He's off in Nashville this week trying to peddle one of the country songs he writes. He's sold three so far and could probably sell more if he'd move to Tennessee. Won't, though. Says he doesn't have the courage. Frankly, I think it's because he can't bear to leave his current sweetie behind." She shook her head slowly. "I have to tell you that I'm continually amazed at how different my two boys are. Randy is too busy socializing to work. Patrick is too busy working to socialize."

Brook thought about that surprising comment for a moment. "What kind of work does he do?" she then asked.

"Patrick? He..." Sarah paused, frowning thoughtfully. "You know, I'm not sure there's a good word for what he does." She held up the night-clothes. "That should be everything. Oops. I forgot the undies. I hope you like bikini panties. That's all Cynthia wears."

"Well, I..."

"How about these?" She held up a pair made of ti-ger-striped satin and a matching wisp of bra. Brooke eyed them with some alarm.

"Uh, perfect," she murmured, but Sarah was al-ready out the door. Brooke scurried after her and in seconds found herself inside a large bathroom.

"Towels are in here. Shampoo and soap on the shelf. I'm sure there's an extra toothbrush in that drawer and toiletries are in that cabinet. Can you think of anything else?"

Brooke, overwhelmed by the woman's unquestion-ing welcome, couldn't possibly. "Not a thing. I really appreciate this."

"Glad to help out. Now I'm going to take these nightclothes on upstairs—Randy's room is to the right—and get busy changing the bed linens."

"I can do that."

"I'd rather you got out of those wet things."

"All right, then."

In seconds Brooke stood alone in the doorway, try-ing to absorb all the information she'd just received.

At that moment Patrick walked by the door, bare-chested and barefoot, headed, most likely, to his room.

He stopped abruptly, as though about to speak. Then his gaze fell on the tiger-striped lingerie lying atop her stack of clothes. He stared at them for a moment, then raised his eyes to meet Brooke's.

"I, um, just met Mom in the hall and she said to tell you that dinner is almost ready. The dining room is downstairs to the left."

"Thanks."

Patrick stood there in silence for another heartbeat, then gave her a brisk nod before turning on his heel to head down the hall with quick steps.

Brooke stared after him, her eyes first on his broad shoulders, then the indentation of his spine, which she trailed clear down to the back pockets of his faded jeans. Utterly fascinated by the movement of those pockets, Brooke barely found wits to shut and lock the door.

Sanity quickly reasserted itself, and she turned on the water, letting it run for only a moment before stepping into the tub. Lying back, Brooke closed her eyes and relished the warmth, swirling therapeutically as it slowly rose around her body.

Then and only then did she allow herself to consider her loss and grieve for it... with great gulping sobs that the running water muffled so Sarah wouldn't hear. That dear woman would naturally want to help her in this time of need and, ever independent, Brooke preferred to solve her problems alone.

Keeping that in mind, she snatched up a washcloth when she finally turned off her tears and the water, scrubbing her face to erase any signs of emotion. That accomplished, she deliberately turned her thoughts to something other than her own precarious situation, namely the occupants of this big ol' house, which were several and diverse.

First she considered Randy, who didn't have the courage to follow his dream to be a songwriter. Then there was Gilbert, who didn't have the heart to face his rehabilitation. Next came Cynthia and her "munch-kins," and, of course, good-hearted Sarah. What an interesting group.

As for Patrick...Brooke didn't know what to make of this man who so generously shared his house and his life with his family. She imagined that wasn't an easy thing to do. He was single, after all—or so she assumed. Having no privacy must be a drag for him.

Clearly he wasn't as big a grump as she'd first thought. All things considered—in particular his kindness to strangers—he might just be a saint. At the least, he was a very nice man, from all appearances maybe even the kind she'd always dreamed of meeting.

Nah, she decided, instantly and instinctively retreating from that thought. Nice men were few and far between. The chances of her meeting one her first day in Texas were almost nil.

And even if he were, she wasn't in the market for a man anymore—even of the "nice" variety. Experience had taught her that flying solo was the only way to travel through this life. That's why she'd cut all ties, loaded up her trailer and come to the Lone Star State in the first place.

Brooke's stomach suddenly growled, reminding her that she hadn't eaten since breakfast. Her mind on the meal that waited downstairs, she soaped up, rinsed down, and stepped out of the tub.

A swipe at the foggy mirror revealed a young woman whose stringy blond hair looked amazingly like hay. With a groan, Brooke grabbed her hairbrush out of her purse and set to work on it. Thanks to that brush and the makeup and cologne in her purse, she looked and felt much better by the time she exited the bathroom in her borrowed finery, still-damp hair pulled back in a single French braid.

Suddenly shy, she walked downstairs, then followed the sound of voices to the dining area. In that brightly illuminated room she found a long table, at which sat all her new friends and a man in a wheelchair, who had to be Gilbert.

"Feeling better?" Sarah asked the moment Brooke stepped through the door.

Brooke, a little daunted by this roomful of people, somehow managed a nod.

"I believe you know everyone but Gilbert. Gilbert, this is Brooke, the young woman we've been telling you about."

The man in question—a strapping, silver-haired specimen with sparkling blue eyes—nodded a greeting, which Brooke returned.

"Now grab yourself a bowl of stew and join us," Sarah then added.

"I'll show you where it is," Patrick said from the doorway behind her. Brooke started at the sound of his voice so close, then stepped quickly aside so he could enter the dining area. Motioning for Brooke to follow him, Patrick walked into what turned out to be a kitchen.

There, he took a blue bowl from the china hutch, then ladled delicious-looking stew into it. The aroma filled the room and Brooke's mouth began to water.

"Is this enough?" Patrick asked, handing it to her.

"For starters," she replied, picking up the bowl. Her thoughtless though candid answer produced a sexy chuckle, and at once her heart began to hammer, a reaction she found astounding.

When their gazes locked, much as they had in the van earlier that evening, Brooke once more noted that strange gleam in his eyes. Attraction? she wondered as she headed back out to the dining table. She hoped her eyes hadn't mirrored that same give-away sparkle. For attracted she found herself . . . and to a man she didn't like very much.

Amazing, she decided as she slipped into an empty chair to eat. Amazing and in keeping with her current run of luck, now that she thought about it. Only two days into a life-impacting decision to pack up and fly solo, she'd already met a man capable of piquing her interest.

"Isn't that right, Brooke?"

Brooke blinked her surprise and looked at her questioner, Sarah, then around the table to find each and every eye on her.

"Oh, uh, y-yes," she stammered, blushing. Then she shrugged rather sheepishly. "I'm sorry. What did you say?"

Everyone laughed, a reaction she surely deserved. Sarah gave her a kind smile. "I told Gilbert that you're moving to Amarillo from Portland."

"I am. Was." Brooke sighed. "Am. First thing tomorrow. I start a new job on Monday and, thanks to that twister, have a lot to do before then."

"What kind of job?" asked Patrick around a mouthful of stew.

"I'm the manager of Ruby's Slipper," she told him, adding, "You know the chain of shoe stores? There's going to be one in Eastgate Mall. Grand opening is—"

"Saturday after next," Patrick said. "I know. I have a business there, too."

"Ruby's Slipper, you say? I don't believe I'm familiar with that chain of stores," commented Sarah, a question that distracted Brooke from asking Patrick what kind of business he was in.

"They're more prevalent up north, I think," Brooke said, going on to share that she had roomed with the daughter of the chain's founder, Ruby Lloyd, in college and from her had learned of the company's manager training program.

"How fortuitous that the man named his daughter that," Sarah said. "Ruby's Slipper is such a clever play on words."

Everyone agreed except Cynthia, who looked rather blank.

"I don't get it," she admitted.

"Oh, Mother," said one of her daughters. Emmy, judging by the blue bow. "Don't you remember Dorothy's ruby slippers in the *Wizard of Oz* book you bought for us? They were all red and shiny."

"And magic," chimed in Shelly.

"Ohh-hh," said Cynthia. She slapped her forehead and then smiled at Brooke. "Sorry. I worked midnight to eight today. I haven't got a brain left in my head."

"Where do you work?" Brooke naturally asked.

"I'm a nurse at Amarillo General. I'm on duty four nights a week in pediatrics. Last night was one of them."

Brooke nodded. "Do you like your job?"

"Love it, and let me tell you there's never a dull moment," Cynthia assured her, following that declaration with several on-the-job anecdotes that kept everyone laughing for the next few minutes.

"What are your plans?" This question came from Gilbert once the mirth died down.

"Immediate? Well, I'm going to call my insurance agent. I'm sure I'm eligible for a rental car and there's the little matter of getting a settlement on my convertible and, if I'm lucky, my other things, too."

Gilbert nodded. "And after that?"

Brooke took note of his concern and was touched. "Once I have wheels, I'll check into a motel and start looking for an apartment, hopefully one that's furnished since I don't have so much as an alarm clock to my name at the moment." For just a second the occupants of the room blurred as Brooke's eyes filled with tears again. Impatiently she blinked them back.

"Patrick can help you there," Cynthia commented, with a smile so sympathetic Brooke suspected she'd seen the telltale emotion. "He owns three pawn shops and a secondhand furniture store."

"He also has six car washes, four Laundromats, a video arcade, and property all over the city," Sarah interjected with obvious pride.

"Really?" Brooke asked Patrick.

He shrugged away the accomplishment. "I find a need and take care of it."

"Own any apartment houses?"

"No. Just parking decks."

"Five of them," Sarah added.

No wonder there wasn't a word for what Patrick did for a living, she thought, watching him out of the corner of her eye. The more she learned about this man, the more of an enigma he became. She wondered again if she might have misjudged him. After all, he'd been nothing but nice to her since their initial face-to-face. Could it be he was just as out of control as she at the time?

Maybe, but the point was moot. Come tomorrow, Brooke would leave—be out of here and never see the man again.

Thank goodness.

After a too generous wedge of apple pie, complete with a scoop of ice cream, Brooke volunteered to clean up.

"Why thank you, dear," Sarah said. "I do have some homework to do tonight."

Homework? Brooke's face must have given away her astonishment since everyone laughed.

"I'm in the accounting program at the community college in Amarillo," Sarah explained, eyes twinkling. "I've always wished I had more education. When I moved in with Patrick last year, he suggested I go for it, so I did. Right now I'm up to my neck in algebra."

"Do you like it?" Brooke asked, rising from her chair and gathering up plates.

Sarah hesitated for just a second, then wrinkled her nose. "Actually, I've found it a bit of a struggle. Cynthia has helped me some, but—"

"It's been eight years since I took algebra," the redhead interjected with a laugh. "And it wasn't my best subject."

"I made A's in algebra and loved it," Brooke heard herself blurt. "I'll tutor you, if you like."

Sarah beamed in response. "Would you?"

"Of course. We could start tonight...?"

"Oh, not tonight. You're exhausted and I just have a few problems to do. But I would like to set up something for later."

"If Brooke's going to manage one of the businesses at the mall, she'll be working from sunup until sundown," Patrick said, also standing to stack dinnerware. "I doubt she'll have time or energy to deal with your algebra."

Sarah's face fell at her son's stern comment. "Oh, dear. What *am* I thinking of? You've got enough on your plate without heaping my problems on it." Her voice spoke volumes of her distress, and Brooke, who already loved the woman, glared at Patrick for causing it.

"I have no intentions of working that hard, and I will have time to help you. Just give me a couple of days to orient, then we'll get busy." That said, Brooke picked up her stack of plates and sashayed to the kitchen.

A second later she was joined by Patrick, carrying a load of his own. He set them on the counter, then reached under the sink to retrieve a rubber mat and a dish rack.

"What are you doing?" Brooke asked, when he next plugged up one of the two sinks, squirted in some dish soap, and turned on the water.

"Helping you wash up."

"That isn't a bit necessary," Brooke replied, more than a little disconcerted at the thought of working shoulder to shoulder with him there in that cozy kitchen.

"Yes, it is. You're a guest and shouldn't be doing this in the first place."

"Washing dishes is small payment for your letting me stay here tonight," Brooke said. "And speaking of that... I intend to pay you for your hospitality, of course.''

''Don't be ridiculous.''

''But—''

''No buts.'' He said those words just the way his mother had earlier, and once again Brooke found herself loath to argue.

So, with an agitated sigh, she nudged Patrick to one side, snatched up a dirty glass, and set it in the hot soapy water. *Very* hot soapy water.

''Ow!'' Brooke exclaimed, jerking her hand back out of the suds and waving it in the air to cool it. Patrick grabbed her wrist and inspected her crimson fingers, then moved the spout over the empty sink and turned on the cold water. After testing it for temperature, he thrust her hand under the cooling flow, a move that forced Brooke to take two stumbling steps forward.

In response, Patrick stepped closer himself and steadied her with his other hand, placed at her waist. He stood so near that his body brushed against hers, contact that Brooke found amazingly stimulating.

So intensely aware of his manly front pressed against her backside was Brooke, that she began to breathe in little pants.

''Are you okay?'' Patrick asked, again inspecting her fingers, an action that told Brooke he'd misconstrued the reason for her agitation.

She opened her mouth to reply, but never got the chance before the swing door burst open and the twins bounded into the room, dirty silverware clutched in their chubby little hands.

"What are you two doing?" Shelly immediately demanded, her wide eyes assessing the situation.

Vastly embarrassed, Brooke tugged her fingers free and twisted away from Patrick.

"I burned my hand," she replied, turning around to face the twins and holding it up for inspection. "Your uncle was trying to make it better."

Both girls hurried forward, deposited their loads on the counter, and minutely examined the injury.

"Does it hurt?" Emmy asked.

"It stings," Brooke admitted.

"Maybe Uncle Patrick needs to kiss it again," Shelly commented. "Sometimes it takes a bunch of them to work."

Brooke felt her cheeks flame and knew they must be darker crimson than her poor old fingers. "Actually, we used cold water on it."

"Then no wonder it still hurts," Emmy commented with a sigh of exasperation. "You need to kiss her fingers, Uncle Patrick. Just like you do mine."

"And quick," Shelly added.

To Brooke's horror, Patrick captured her hand in his again and loudly kissed every finger. By the time he finished his gentle ministrations, she could barely breathe and her legs felt as supportive as wet noodles.

"That'll do," she blurted, yanking her hand free. "Doesn't hurt a bit now."

"Let me see," Emmy said, tugging on Brooke's sleeve and rising on tiptoe to make another inspection.

"They're still awfully red," she announced. "Maybe he needs to work on them some more."

"Oh, no," Brooke hastily argued. "That's plenty of kisses. Plenty. I'll be just fine now."

"She sure will," Patrick said. "And just to be sure, I'll keep an eye on her, okay?"

"Well...okay." That from Emmy, who was clearly reluctant to drop the issue. Brooke heaved a mental sigh of relief and wished that the girls would take their curious eyes somewhere else.

"Don't you two have something to do?" Patrick asked, clearly wishing the same thing.

"Uh-uh," Shelly told him.

"Are you sure? My watch says eight o'clock. Isn't that your bedtime?"

"We can stay up until eight-thirty on Friday night," Emmy informed him in a very grown-up way. "You know that."

"So you can. So you can. Well then, I'll tell you what. You two run on upstairs and get ready for bed. And just as soon as I finish in here, I'll be up to read to you."

"The Wizard of Oz?"

"Again?"

Both girls nodded.

"Then the *Wizard of Oz* it is. Now scoot."

They did . . . much to Brooke's relief. Gratefully she turned back to the sink, only to be set aside by Patrick. He directed the spout back over to the other sink with a slap and then added cold water to the hot already in it.

After testing the water temperature, he began to wash dishes, handing them to Brooke one by one as he finished each. They worked in silence, a state of affairs that suited Brooke just fine. And the minute the task was complete, she folded the towel and headed toward the swing door that separated the kitchen from the rest of the house.

"There's a phone in my office on the third floor," Patrick said before she could escape through that door.

"Excuse me?" She paused, but didn't bother to turn around.

"You want to call your insurance company, don't you?"

Damn. She'd forgotten all about that. "Yes. Of course. Third floor, you say?"

"That's right. Across from Randy's room, where you'll sleep tonight."

"Thanks," Brooke murmured, then slipped outside and headed in that direction. She found the room without any trouble since there were only two in the attic.

Unable to resist a quick peek at where she would sleep, Brooke flipped on the light and stepped through the door.

Though clearly a man's room—rich, bold colors, paneled walls, wildlife photographs everywhere—a woman's touch was evident here and there. Brooke took special delight in the king-size bed with its four posters and bedknobs the size of cannonballs. How nice it would be to curl up under that fluffy quilt.

Every bone in her body suddenly ached, but she ignored the fatigue. Phone call first, then that much-needed rest.

Turning, Brooke walked across the hall to the office. She switched that light on, too, and inspected the area with interest. To her left she found a desk, complete with computer and printer, telephone, and huge stacks of papers, all shapes and sizes. To her right, she saw a packed bookcase and two file cabinets.

A very ordinary office, she decided, walking on inside to where a cane room divider stood, blocking her view of the rest of the area. Brooke peeked around it and smiled when she discovered a well-worn couch, a television set, a VCR and a stereo.

"My hideaway," Patrick said from behind her, words that gave Brooke quite a start and made her wonder if he was part cat. He sure knew how to get around without being heard.

Turning, a hand to her thumping heart, she found herself eyes-to-chin with him. "Sorry. I didn't mean to snoop."

"That's okay. Did you get hold of your insurance agent?"

"Actually, I've been exploring. You have a lovely house, Patrick."

"Think so?" He looked rather pleased by the compliment.

"Mmm-hmm. I can't imagine what you ever did all alone in it, though. I mean, it's huge."

"Exactly the reason I've rounded up my family... that and the fact that they all had a need at the moment—"

"And you take care of needs."

"That's right." He stood perfectly still, his gaze intent and a little disconcerting. "Do you have a need, Brooke? Is there something else I can do for you besides loaning you a roof for the night?"

Yipes! Had the man guessed his effect on her nerves, her body, her libido?

"I've got everything under control," she lied. "Or will have as soon as I make these calls."

Patrick nodded solemnly, his expression unreadable. "Then why don't I let you get to it?" He moved to the door.

"What about you?" Brooke heard herself ask, a question that halted him dead in this tracks. "Sometimes men who see after the needs of others forget their own. Do you have a need, Patrick Sawyer? You won't let me pay you money for staying here tonight. May I repay you another way? Is there, perhaps, something *I* can do for *you?*"

Patrick turned very slowly. He studied her for a second, then walked back with steps as quick as Brooke's heartbeat.

"My needs are few," he told her when they stood inches apart. "A roof over my head, my family around me, a new business venture now and then.

There's nothing whatsoever you—or any woman—can do for me, Brooke Brady.''

That said, he strode from the room and shut the door behind him, creating a breeze that chilled her as much as his words.

Chapter Three

It took thirty minutes for Brooke to turn her automobile problems over to an insurance agent. She used the toll-free telephone number printed on her card, not for the first time sending heavenward a thanks that she'd had the wits to grab her purse earlier that day when she took shelter from the tornado.

Secure in the knowledge that she would have wheels again by tomorrow, Brooke walked across the hall to Randy's bedroom. She slipped gratefully out of Cynthia's jeans, which were too long and too tight, and the blouse that hugged her chest and gaped between the buttons.

The bra was a joy to abandon, too. Of the underwire variety, it cut into Brooke's ribs and pushed her breasts up under her neck—at least that was what it felt like. In reality, she knew she'd looked okay in the clothes, but it would be good to wear her own again. Sarah had promised to wash them tonight.

After stretching her weary limbs, Brooke pulled the nylon gown on over her head. Pink and pretty, it fit much better than the other borrowed finery, though it was, like the blouse and bra, a little snug in the bust.

With a sigh of pure pleasure, Brooke crawled between the crisp floral sheets on Randy's big bed and snuggled down under the comforter. Immediately one thousand and one worries filled her head, not the least among them replacing her clothes and her personal belongings, finding an apartment, and starting her new job.

Brooke sighed again, this time with weariness. Pushing her worries to the back of her mind, she purposefully recalled the pleasurable aspects of her drive down from Oregon. She remembered the many rivers, the varied terrain, the road winding to forever.

She thought about the wildlife she'd seen, the people she'd met, the towheaded toddler who'd offered her bubblegum at a rest stop somewhere along the way.

Smiling at that particular memory, Brooke gave in to her fatigue and drifted off to dream of... freight trains. Roaring trains that sped down crisscrossed tracks pursued by tornadoes. Dozens of tornadoes. Swirling, black, reaching from heaven to hell and wreaking havoc on red cars.

With a gasp of sheer terror, Brooke jerked awake. Her heart thumped painfully in her chest and loudly

in her ears. She shivered, huddled further under the
blankets and breathed deeply for several seconds, all
the while reassuring herself that she was safe and
sound . . . safe and sound. . . .

It took a whole fifteen minutes for Brooke to calm
down enough to doze again. This time she dreamed of
that old tree in the backyard of her father's Seattle,
Washington, mansion . . . the one up which a thunder-
storm had caught her some twenty years ago. As had
happened then, the wind began to blow quite suddenly, shaking the branches until she didn't dare try to
climb down. Then the rain started, and the lighten-
ing, and, of course, the thunder.

But here the events of that particular afternoon
changed and in tonight's dreamscape Brooke faced
another menace—a tornado—that dropped down
from the sky and plucked her favorite tree from that
neatly landscaped backyard with its brick privacy
fence, swimming pool and well-tended flower gar-
dens. The tree began to spin wildly. She clung to the
branches, screaming her terror.

Abruptly, Brooke woke again, this time lightly
beaded with cold sweat. She sucked fresh air into her
laboring lungs and tossed the covers aside. Sitting up,
she swung her feet to the parquet floor and just stood
there for a moment, heart once again thumping like
crazy.

Clearly there would be no sleep for her this night.
Bone-weary or not.

Brooke turned on a bedside lamp and glanced at her
watch, noting that it was only just past midnight.

Restlessly she began to pace the room, looking for a magazine or a book to read. She found nothing that interested her in the least, and as far as she could find, there was no television or radio, either.

Another five minutes of prowling found Brooke near wit's end. Then, suddenly inspired, she snatched up the borrowed robe, slipped it on and headed to the office across the hall, where she remembered seeing a television.

Brooke hesitated outside the closed door, but only for a second since no light could be seen spilling out from under it. She entered the room and turned right around to ease the door back shut, only then hearing the voice.

Her heart slammed into her chest. She whirled around to find her host seated on the narrow couch at the back of the room and looking downright sinister, bathed as he was in the silvery glow of the television.

"Whatsamatter?" he drawled. "Can't sleep?"

Brooke, whose eyes had finally adjusted to the dim light in the room, nodded in reply, all the while wrapping her robe more securely about her. She fumbled for a belt, and when she didn't find one, had to settle for clutching the front together with her hand.

"I'm so sorry. If I'd known you were in here I'd never have..." Belatedly Brooke realized how that might sound.

"Come in?" Patrick laughed without humor. "Am I such an ogre?"

"You're not an ogre at all," Brooke replied, too polite to insult this man who'd so freely opened his house to her. "What I meant was—"

"I know what you meant," he said in a tone so cool she suspected he really did. At once, Brooke rued her inability to hide her true feelings. That transparency had gotten her into trouble more than once.

"Mind if I join you?" she asked in an attempt to hide her opinion of him. He *was,* after all, Sarah's son and *her* host. "I've had a couple of nightmares tonight and I'm feeling sort of spooked."

"Battle shock?" Patrick shifted his gaze from the television, scanned her expression, then scooted to one side on the two-cushion couch. "Sure. Have a seat." He patted the unoccupied one.

Brooke walked on into the room and sat down next to him. "What are you watching?"

"Alien."

"Oh, that should do wonders for my nerves," she commented, thoughtless words that actually made Patrick chuckle. That sound, surprisingly warm, shimmied right down her spine. Immediately the tension in the room lessened.

"We could watch something else." Patrick reached for the remote control. "Seems like there's an old John Wayne movie on Channel Twenty. Can't remember which."

"But you were already into *Alien,*" Brooke protested, flattered but appalled that he would abandon his movie for her.

"I've seen it before." He flipped through the channels in rapid-fire succession, halting when a golden two-zero lit up on the lower right-hand corner of the screen. "Looks like it's *Hatari!*. One of my favorites. Have you seen it?"

"Just a couple of dozen times," Brooke replied around a yawn. "And it's exactly what I need tonight. Thanks."

He shrugged in reply and handed her a bowl of popcorn heretofore unnoticed. "Hungry?"

"Always," she admitted, taking the bowl.

They watched the movie in silence, then, the two of them. Brooke ate a goodly portion of the popcorn, assisted by Patrick. To her surprise, she felt relaxed, shockingly at home. And having seen the film so many times, her attention naturally strayed . . . back to that last nightmare, the one that took place in her father's yard.

What would that parent say if he knew her current situation? Brooke couldn't help but wonder. Would he worry about his only child? Would he, perhaps, fly to Emerald City to rescue her? Would he take her back home with him?

Home? Not a home. Just a very large house wherein now lived his too young wife and the nine-year-old stepson he'd talked about ad nauseam at the banquet honoring Brooke's graduation from manager training just last week.

Brooke had listened politely to his tales of Boy Scouts, Little League, and football, dying inside with every word. If the past twenty years of nannies, housekeepers, and fatherly neglect weren't enough to convince her that Jonathan Brady didn't love her, then his bragging about a boy who wasn't even flesh-and-blood kin certainly was.

That truth had hurt at the time, but it had also spurred her to accept this Texas job offer—to cut ties, to begin again. And though a difficult decision— Brooke had also been offered a position in Seattle— she knew it was the right one.

So what if things weren't going wonderfully well right this moment. There was always tomorrow....

"Brooke?" Patrick whispered his guest's name, not wanting to wake her if she actually dozed.

She never moved, just sat there with her chin propped on her hand, her elbow propped on the arm-rest and her eyes closed. Her soft, steady breathing reinforced his belief that she'd finally fallen asleep, and Patrick settled back to watch her do it.

Beginning with her honey-blond hair, he let his gaze travel over every inch of this woman, this Brooke Brady, who had turned his life topsy-turvy.

He noted her upturned nose, lightly sprinkled with freckles, her mouth, so kissable, and her skin, look-ing silky soft and slightly flushed. She had a slender, graceful neck, and below that, a body designed to drive a man wild.

Patrick couldn't see much of that body, covered as it was by Cynthia's old blue robe, but he really didn't need to. Simply being this close to Brooke set him on fire, and the sexy scent of her cologne fanned the flames.

Immediate and incredible, this heated reaction, not to mention unprecedented, unexpected and un-wanted. Thank goodness Brooke would be leaving to-morrow. Another day or two more in her presence might mean the death of him, and Patrick had no de-sire to be cremated.

He did have other desires, though—desires long denied; desires that now haunted him with a ven-geance. He found himself yearning for...what? Brooke?

Not Brooke, he quickly told himself. Not necessar-ily Brooke.

But female companionship for sure...and no wonder. He hadn't dated seriously in more than two years. He hadn't dated *period* in more than six months. And all because of Stephanie, the fiancée from hell. Why, just remembering the way that woman treated his family raised Patrick's blood pressure.

As for how she treated him....

Thinking back, he couldn't remember what he ever saw in her. Well, Patrick grinned to himself, maybe he *could,* but for all her womanly charms, she wasn't nearly as enticing as Brooke.

Brooke? Enticing? Patrick snapped to attention and settled his gaze on his sleeping companion's face. She stirred restlessly and made a sort of sighing sound that touched and worried him all at once.

Was she dreaming again? Cold? Uncomfortable?

Ever so quietly, Patrick eased off the couch and squatted down on the floor in front of her. Gently he clasped her shoulders and maneuvered her to where she lay on her side, head on a sofa pillow. She sighed, then curled up, but didn't wake.

Grinning at his success, Patrick stretched over to retrieve the much-used afghan his mother had crocheted for him a couple of birthdays ago. He spread it over Brooke, then sat back on his heels, once more watching her sleep.

She stirred again, frowned and brushed a hand over her face, but never once opened her eyes. Concerned that she might wake, Patrick leaned forward, intending to push back the strand of hair lying across her cheek—hair that must tickle.

At that moment the television blared the high-adventure musical score, catching Patrick unawares. He jumped in response and accidentally touched Brooke's cheek.

Her eyes flew open. She gasped, then shoved hard at Patrick, a move that tipped him over on his backside onto the plush carpet.

"What are you doing?" she demanded, leaping up to glare down at her bewildered host.

"You fell asleep, so I—" Abruptly Brooke's outrage registered, along with a possible reason for it. His jaw dropped. His cheeks flamed. "Surely you don't think..."

"Think? I know." That said, Brooke wrapped her robe tightly across her body and swept past him, five feet two inches of righteous indignation.

Patrick sprang up and grabbed her arm, halting her. "I'd never lay a hand on you."

"Oh yeah?" she retorted, her pointed gaze on her captured wrist.

He let go instantly and tried another defense. "Contrary to what you obviously think, I'm not the kind of guy who takes advantage of sleeping women."

"Not enough challenge for you?" Her eyes tossed daggers of dislike straight at his heart.

And though wounded by them, Patrick held onto his composure. "Let's just say I've never found snoring particularly appealing."

"I do not snore!"

Patrick allowed himself one "Oh yeah?" shrug in reply.

With a strangled oath, Brooke snatched up the sofa pillow and threw it at him. Then she dashed for the door.

"You're worse than any ogre," she announced just before she exited. "You're a...a...*jerk*." A heartbeat later, the door clicked shut behind her, a sound that set Patrick's teeth on edge almost as much as the last insult she hurled.

Patrick fumed about her unjust opinion of him every waking moment that night. He still fumed when he walked downstairs the next morning, two hours later than he usually did on Saturdays. Fully intending to reopen the issue of ogres and jerks, he wasted not a moment, but looked all around for Brooke. The only person he found was Gilbert, seated in the kitchen, his nose stuck in the newspaper.

"Morning," Patrick said to him.

His uncle merely grunted in reply and never took his eyes off the printed pages before him.

"Where is everyone?" Patrick then asked, undaunted by Gilbert's less-than-welcoming demeanor. He wasn't a morning person, either.

"Sarah and the twins are at the grocery store. Cynthia's running an errand. Randy's in Nashville."

As if Patrick didn't know *that*. "And Brooke?"

"Who?"

"Our guest."

"Ah. The blonde with the million-dollar smile."

"She's blond, all right," Patrick murmured. "But I really haven't noticed the smile."

Now Gilbert lowered his paper. He peered at Patrick over his bifocals—the half-moon kind, perched on the end of his nose.

"I'm not a bit surprised," he murmured somewhat dryly. "Especially after what I heard at midnight last night."

So that was it. Gilbert, who slept below the office, had overheard the argument and now sided with Brooke.

Traitor.

"Where is she, Uncle Gil?" Patrick asked, refusing to be intimidated by his crusty old relative.

With a sigh and a shake of his head, Gilbert directed his attention back to his newspaper. "She's the errand Cynthia's running. They've gone to pick up her rental car."

"So they'll be coming back here?"

"I couldn't say for sure, but I really doubt it. Brooke seemed rather eager to shake the dust of thirty-five Baumgartner off her feet. Why, I can't imagine." He lowered the paper a scant half inch and gave Patrick another look of censure.

"Well, neither can I," his nephew snapped, spinning on his heel to stalk from the room.

Patrick spent the next hour reading the *Wall Street Journal* in the living room with the window open so he could listen for Cynthia's and Brooke's return. When he finally heard the slam of a car door, he dashed through the front entrance without even looking out, only to discover that it was Sarah and the girls who'd come home, not Brooke and Cynthia.

Patrick took over transferring the bags of food indoors while the females went inside to put everything away. Just as he reached in the mini-van for the last bag, Cynthia wheeled into the drive. Mere moments later, a conservative white sedan did the same.

From it leaped Brooke, dressed in her own clothes and clearly excited—probably because she would soon be on her way to Amarillo and far away from the "jerk" who'd attacked her last night.

Patrick found that bothered him more than he cared to admit . . . probably because he wasn't a jerk.

So why are you acting like one? a still, small voice asked from the back forty of his mind.

"I'm not," Patrick muttered aloud, just as Cynthia passed by him en route to the house.

"Not what?" She eyed him with open curiosity.

"Not anything." He growled the words, not for the first time in the past twenty-four hours venting his irritation with himself on an innocent bystander.

"Well, who spit in your cornflakes?" Cynthia retorted without batting an eye. Clearly big bro didn't intimidate her one bit. "Or are you just upset because Brooke is leaving?"

"Don't be an idiot." That said, Patrick stomped to the house and deposited his load on the kitchen table with the other things.

A second later, Cynthia and Brooke came indoors, too. Instantly the twins stampeded them and rained questions on Brooke.

"Did you get your new car?"

"Can we ride in it?"

"Yes and yes...sort of," said Brooke. "It's not mine exactly, and I can't take you for a ride today. I have an appointment with my insurance agent in—" she glanced at her watch "—forty-five minutes. I'm afraid I have to hit the road." She turned to Sarah, who stood nearby with a can of green beans in each hand.

"Thanks for everything," Brooke said, stepping forward to give the woman a hug—beans and all—and a kiss on the cheek.

"I'm glad to help out."

Brooke smiled at her, then turned to Gilbert, who'd rolled his chair into the dining room, no doubt to check out the commotion.

"I really enjoyed our little chat this morning," she told him.

They'd had a chat?

"So did I," Gilbert replied, accepting the hug Brooke gave him as well as the kiss she placed on his forehead.

Brooke next said her good-byes to the sad-faced twins by presenting them with a lollipop apiece. "The man at that little store on the corner told me these were your favorite kind," she said before hugging and kissing each child in turn.

They returned the embrace, showering her with the kid-size affection Patrick had come to appreciate since they'd moved in with him not so long ago.

Cynthia was hugged next and she, too, received a kiss on the cheek before Brooke turned to Patrick. By now well aware of how Brooke Brady said goodbye, Patrick actually tensed. Was he going to get a hug and kiss, too?

At the mere thought, his libido screamed "Pleeeeze . . . !"

But all Brooke gave Patrick was her hand.

"Thanks for loaning me Randy's room," she said, her voice cool, her tone formal.

"No problem," Patrick replied just as stiffly as he took, shook and released the proffered hand.

"Are you mad at Uncle Patrick?" The question came from Emily, now standing at Brooke's elbow.

"What makes you say that?" Brooke asked her.

"You treated him different."

Brooke hesitated fractionally—or did Patrick imagine it?—before stepping up to wrap her arms

around him in a very quick hug that involved nothing
but her arms.

"There now," she said as she stepped back. "Satisfied?"

Emmy nodded, but her sister did not.

"You have to *kiss* him, too," Shelly said. "Just like
you did the rest of us."

That suggestion, spoken with a five-year-old's sincerity, reminded Patrick of last night in the kitchen. A
kiss had been requested by his precocious nieces then,
as well, and he'd gladly obliged. Would Brooke be as
accommodating? he wondered even as she stood on
tiptoe to touch her lips to the dimple in his left cheek.

Patrick felt the aftershock of that brief, brushing
kiss clear to his toes. Before he could recover from it,
Brooke stepped back and turned to the twins. "Are
you two happy now?"

Emmy again nodded immediately, but Shelly still
wasn't so sure. "Girls and boys are supposed to kiss
on the mouth."

"Michele Renee Kimbrell!" scolded Cynthia, her
voice shocked, her eyes twinkling.

"Well, they are," Shelly insisted while her ever-
hopeful uncle stood ready... just in case he got lucky
and Brooke agreed.

Brooke didn't. "But what about Gilbert?" she
asked instead. "I didn't kiss him on the mouth."

"Oh, he's old," Shelly replied, discounting her
great-uncle with an airy wave of her hand.

"He is not old," Brooke argued, clearly as amused
as everyone in the room except, maybe, Uncle Gil-

bert. "And age has nothing to do with it, anyway. Remember last night in the kitchen? Patrick kissed my *fingers,* didn't he?"

"Only 'cause they were hurt," Shelly stated. "That doesn't count."

"Sure it does," Brooke said, words with which Cynthia and Sarah didn't necessarily agree if the telling look they exchanged was anything to go by.

Though Shelly opened her mouth to argue, she never got the chance. For at that moment Gilbert growled and captured her in his strong arms. Squealing as she ducked his whiskery chin, Shelly promptly forgot her preoccupation with kissing.

Brooke, who stood with one foot already out the door, looked infinitely relieved and past ready to go, Patrick thought, especially now that his mother and sister watched the two of them so closely. For that reason, he wasn't a bit surprised when she didn't wait for the laughter to die down before she waved to everyone and beat a hasty retreat, calling, "Later."

Unlike the night before, Patrick felt nothing when the door shut behind her this time. But when he heard the car's engine roar to life a few moments later, something very like gloom settled over him.

Baffled, Patrick shook his head, exited the kitchen and slowly climbed the stairs to his office and all the work piled on his desk.

It was high time to get back to normal again, he told himself. Brooke had stolen fifteen—no, sixteen— hours of his life. That was more than he'd spared any woman in more than a year and all this particular one was going to get.

"'Out of sight, out of mind,' that's my motto," Patrick muttered aloud with conviction, pushing open the door of his office and stepping into the room.

Instantly the lingering scent of her cologne assailed him, a vivid reminder that "sight" was only one of his five senses.

As for the others—smell, touch, taste and hear—something told him those just might make forgetting Brooke Brady the challenge of a lifetime.

Chapter Four

The minute Patrick's house disappeared from view behind her, Brooke heaved a lusty sigh of pure relief. Good-byes were never easy, and for a child raised by strangers, hugs and kisses weren't, either.

But she'd managed them, and she would almost bet that none of the recipients of said hugs and kisses suspected how uncomfortable they made her feel. In fact, such an idea would probably never cross their minds, as used as they were to loving hellos and good-byes. Brooke had observed her new friends closely while in their company and taken her cue from them—thus, the mandatory farewell ceremony.

Now that she had that stressful business behind her, she was ready to turn her full attention to what lay ahead: Amarillo. Brooke had much to do before she reported to work on Monday. The sooner she got busy, the better.

First on her list, of course, was the meeting with her auto insurance agent. They had arranged to get together at a fast-food restaurant on the outskirts of Amarillo to reimburse Brooke for the rental vehicle. There, too, she would fill out the forms necessary to have her car removed from Patrick's car wash.

Patrick.

Brooke winced as he crashed into her consciousness. How long had she successfully held thoughts of him at bay? Three miles? Four? Then *pow!* There he was—on her mind.

Brooke found herself reliving what had been a very embarrassing good-bye. She felt once again the roughness of his unshaved cheek against her lips. She smelled once again the spicy scent of his after-shave. Her heart hammered anew.

Darn, but the man had sex appeal.

Too bad he was such a jerk.

And he was a jerk—with a capital J. Why else would he have attacked her the night before?

Attacked? Not exactly, but he had knelt so close to the couch and touched her face....

Very disconcerting behavior, that, as disconcerting as her own pretense of sleep when, in reality, she'd been wide awake from the moment he'd tucked the afghan around her. Could it be she'd unconsciously invited his caress . . . hoped for it, even?

With a shake of her head to clear it of embarrassing deceptions and unanswered questions, Brooke dragged her thoughts back to her list and the second "to do" on it: check into a motel. Third was finding a mall, where she would take care of items four through whatever it took to bathe, dress, eat, do her hair and otherwise subsist.

So much to do! Her spirits plummeted in the face of it.

But those spirits, never down for long, soared again only moments later when Brooke spied the restaurant where her insurance agent, by prearrangement, waited to clear up yesterday's mess.

And by the time Brooke guided her car down that exit ramp, she hummed along with the radio, knowing that whatever lay ahead couldn't be as bad as what lay behind.

Barely two hours later found Brooke in a dress shop in Center City Mall. On one arm hung a shopping bag filled with the essentials she'd purchased from the various establishments in this shopper's paradise. Tucked under the other were assorted boxes that held enough color-coordinated skirts, jackets and blouses to mix, match and otherwise get her through a week.

From her shoulder dangled her faithful purse, in which lay a credit card for an account now charged to within dollars of the limit. Fortunately, all she lacked was a good, comfortable pair of shoes. Unfortunately, Amarillo didn't boast a Ruby's Slipper... yet... so she would have to buy them elsewhere.

Brooke hated that and not just because she didn't want to patronize her competition. Having worked for

Ruby's Slipper for years beginning part-time as a student in college, she appreciated top quality at affordable prices. Her belief that others did, too, provided her with confidence and enthusiasm, two traits essential if she was to succeed as manager of the Amarillo store.

Another essential trait would be energy—something Brooke was fresh out of by the time she returned to her motel room around three o'clock that afternoon. A chilly blast of air greeted her upon entry, so the moment she rid herself of her purchases she made a beeline for the air conditioner to adjust the temperature. Then she went back out and bought a newspaper from the box she'd seen outside the motel office when she'd checked in earlier.

Though tempted to get started at once on her apartment hunt, Brooke took the time to hang up her new clothes so they wouldn't wrinkle. She next called out for pizza, then and only then allowing herself to stretch out across the bed and study the classified ads of the *Amarillo Daily*.

If Brooke had any worries about the availability of apartments, she forgot them the moment she began to peruse the ads, circling anything that sounded even remotely suited to her needs. As it turned out, there were several. Now all she had to do was find one in a nice part of town, preferably near Eastgate Mall.

On that thought, Brooke sat up and retrieved her purse from the bedside table. From it, she extracted a Texas map, on which she remembered seeing a detail of Amarillo streets. She quickly realized it would assist her in no way except getting around the city. Clearly she would have to enlist the help of a local if she wanted to do any smart renting.

Since Brooke only knew six people in Texas, she had no trouble figuring out who to call for help: Cynthia. That decided, she dug her notepad out of her purse— the one with Cynthia's phone number on it—and dialed up her new friend.

One of the twins answered the phone in a deceptively grown-up voice and in seconds Cynthia was on the line and listening to Brooke's plea.

"I'd love to help you," Cynthia said. "But I've only lived in the area six months, and *that* after years and years away. You need someone with a little more expertise. You need Patrick."

"Oh, not Patrick," Brooke exclaimed, cringing at the very thought of spending time with him. "How about Sarah?"

"Mother's a dear, but she knows nothing about the city or renting apartments. You really need Patrick. No one knows the streets of Amarillo better than he does."

"I wouldn't feel comfortable asking him."

"You won't have to," Cynthia said. "I'll do it. *Yo, Bro!* Can you com'ere a minute?"

Brooke winced and suddenly wondered why she hadn't just called a real estate company. That would have been a more logical move for a woman who called herself independent . . .

"Hello."

"Oh, um, hi," Brooke's voice sounded breathless even to her own ears. "H-how are you?" *How are you?* What a question to ask of a man who'd been in the prime of health only five hours ago.

"I'm all right. You?"

"Fine. Just fine," she lied. "I was, um, wondering... What I mean is..." *Well, darn.* "Did Cynthia tell you what I need?"

"Uh-huh, and I'm free tomorrow afternoon. How about you?"

"Tomorrow...?" His easy acquiescence caught her off guard. "Why, yes. Thanks."

"Do you have some apartments in mind?"

"I have circled a few in the classifieds."

"Tell me your price range."

She did.

"All right. Why don't I do a little circling of my own and we'll compare notes. Where are you staying?"

She told him.

"Shall I pick you up at, say, one o'clock?"

"You really don't mind?"

"Nah. I owe you."

He owed her? "Excuse me?"

But it was Cynthia on the line now. "Wasn't that easy? And finding an apartment will be, too. Patrick is a wizard at that sort of thing."

A wizard? Try scientist... of the Dr. Jekyll-Mr. Hyde variety. And for that reason, Brooke sat and pondered Patrick's comment about *owing her* for some time after she hung up the phone.

Did he mean he owed her for smashing his car wash? Or did he want to make amends for his behavior the night before?

Brooke admitted she knew too little about Patrick Sawyer to say for sure, but nonetheless believed he could be trusted. Last night she'd told the man she didn't appreciate his advances. This morning he'd kept his distance.

That, if anything, told her that Patrick was the "nice" man she'd long suspected him to be.

And who better than one of those—especially one familiar with Amarillo—to help her find an apartment?

Patrick knocked on Brooke's door at one o'clock sharp on Sunday, but only because he circled the block for ten minutes so he wouldn't arrive early.

She answered his knock in seconds, pulling open the door, flashing that million-dollar smile Uncle Gil had told him about. Patrick felt an instant flash of jealousy that another man had basked in its glow—even that "old" man who was really quite handsome and had a reputation as a smoothie with the ladies.

Such jealousy was ridiculous, he reminded himself as he accepted Brooke's invitation to come inside. Almost as ridiculous as the joy he experienced when Brooke asked his help in finding an apartment. That seemed to say she'd forgiven him for attacking her.

Attacking? Not by a long shot, though in retrospect his actions Friday night were every bit as inexcusable if unpremeditated. He'd had no business touching her—wouldn't again—even though she looked too utterly enticing in that colorful sundress she wore today.

No, he'd keep his distance from now on. Any moves would be hers.

On that outrageous thought, Patrick actually laughed, a sound that prompted Brooke to tip her head to one side and study him.

"What's so funny?" she asked.

"Oh, uh, *that,*" he blurted, hastily indicating the multitude of bags and boxes piled in one corner of the room. "Been shopping, I see."

"Have I ever," Brooke replied, rolling her expressive hazel eyes. "It's tough starting from scratch. I had to buy *everything.*" She walked over to the bed and sat on the foot of it, indicating that Patrick should occupy the one and only chair. "I just hope I can find a furnished apartment."

"If you don't, and even if you do, remember that I can probably help you out with anything extra you might need."

"Thanks," Brooke said, flashing that smile again. "But I'm up to here—" she tapped the underside of her chin with the back of her fingers "—in debt at the moment. I'll make do with what I have."

"I meant I'd loan you whatever you need," Patrick said. "I have a warehouse full of stuff—some of it antique, some of it just plain old. You can help yourself."

She didn't answer for a moment, but scrutinized him with disconcerting intensity. "Why would you do that for me, Patrick? We barely know each other, after all. I could be a thief.''

A good point, that, and one to which he had no response—at least not a response he wanted to share with her. "You look honest enough to me," he therefore said. "And don't forget my fascination with needs...."

"Ah, yes," she said, her gaze now somewhere on the carpet between them. "Your supply-and-demand principle. I'll keep it in mind."

"And call if you need anything?"

"Yes." She raised her gaze to his, her expression so solemn that Patrick found himself wondering if this seemingly light conversation had a deeper meaning for her, as well.

But of course not.

"Here are the apartments I thought sounded good," Brooke said, reaching for a folded newspaper.

Shaking himself out of his trance, Patrick retrieved his own newspaper from the back pocket of his khaki shorts. He unfolded it, then moved his chair closer to the bed so they could compare choices.

A quick scan of hers revealed her ignorance of Amarillo. She'd circled several that were, to his way of thinking, on the wrong side of the tracks. Amarillo, though a respectable city, was just like any other in the good ol' U.S.A. and could boast both safe and unsafe neighborhoods.

Patrick wanted to be sure Brooke lived in a safe one and so took her paper and proceeded with enthusiasm to cross out any and all that weren't. When he finished, he looked up to find her watching him.

"What are you doing?" she demanded, snatching back the newspaper and scanning it with visible dismay.

"Marking off the apartments that aren't suitable."

"But that only leaves—" she counted them "—seven."

"So it does," he replied, getting to his feet. He handed her the phone. "Why don't you call and set us up some appointments to look them over. I'm going to get a Coke from that machine outside." He strode over to the door, which he unlocked before exiting. "Want one?"

Brooke, her eyes still on the classifieds, answered him with the briefest of nods, sighed, and began to dial.

Patrick deliberately took his time about getting the soft drinks. When he returned with them some fifteen minutes later, he found Brooke still on the telephone. She wrote something down, murmured a thank-you, then hung up.

"All done. One was taken. I have appointments for the other six, though."

Patrick handed her the canned drink. "And the first is . . . ?"

"In forty-five minutes." She showed him which ad. "I wasn't sure how far we'd have to drive."

"Actually, we're only a couple of miles from that apartment complex, but that'll give us time for a minitour. Ready?"

"Sure," she replied with a shrug, gathering up her newspaper and her straw purse, then heading to the door. Outside, they argued over who would drive until Brooke pointed out that the experience would help her become more familiar with the city.

Grumbling under his breath, Patrick gave up and got into her rental car. He had to let back the seat to accommodate his long legs, but was comfortable enough and soon grateful for the opportunity to look instead of drive.

And look he did . . . at Brooke as she guided the car to his directions. She wore her hair down today and curled on the ends. Natural curl? he wondered, barely resisting the urge to touch it. Emmy and Shelly both had natural curls. Soft-as-silk curls that he loved to mess up almost as much as they hated for him to do it.

"You're laughing again," Brooke commented, glancing over at him. "Is my driving so bad?"

"You're driving is fine," he replied, going on to explain his recent thought process. He left out the part about wanting to touch her curls, of course.

"So Emmy and Shelly have natural curl, huh?" Brooke said. She added a pout that turned him inside out. "Lucky them. I don't have a bit."

"But what about this?" Patrick said, making the most of this opportunity to tug on her hair. It was every bit as silky as his nieces'.

"That, my friend, is courtesy of my brand-new hot rollers."

Her friend? Instantly, Patrick's head filled with a vision of Brooke, sitting on her bed dressed in—

what?—with curlers in her hair. He was sorry he hadn't been there to watch. Sorry he was just a friend she called when she needed help to find an apartment.

He believed he might rather share one with her . . . but only for a night, of course. That should be enough to cure his blues.

"Naturally curly or not, your hair is beautiful," he said from the heart.

She looked honestly surprised, and leaned over slightly to view herself in the rearview mirror.

"You think?" she murmured, even as the right front wheel of the car scraped the curb. With a gasp and a charming blush, Brooke righted the vehicle. "Sorry. Where to now?"

"Left," Patrick instructed, getting briskly back to business. All these thoughts of bedrooms and hair curlers did nothing for his peace of mind . . . or body. "And now left again."

Brooke did as directed, turning into a parking lot, halting near a building with a door marked Manager.

"Want me to go in with you?" Patrick asked in a show of tact about as natural as Brooke's curls.

"You can suit yourself," she replied, adding, "but I wouldn't mind a second opinion."

Since Patrick always had one of those, he leaped right out of her car and walked inside the office with her. A few minutes and questions later found the two of them following the apartment manager up two flights of stairs to the tiniest apartment Patrick had ever seen.

While Brooke and the man toured the kitchen and bedroom, Patrick perused the living room, barely large enough to accommodate a love seat, a chair and maybe one end table. The wallpaper sported a huge water stain, as did the ceiling.

He frowned, not a bit pleased with what he saw.

One look at Brooke's expression revealed that she wasn't any more impressed, and in minutes they were back in the car.

"Can you believe he's asking five-fifty for that dollhouse?" she murmured in obvious disgust as she started the engine.

Patrick couldn't. "Maybe the next one will be better."

"I hope so," she said with a smile now worth maybe half a mil.

That smile went steadily bankrupt as the afternoon wore on and they found apartment after apartment unsuitable. Finally they were down to two.

From her vantage point behind the steering wheel of her car, Brooke peered through the windshield at the quaint frame building before them.

White with yellow shutters, the two-story structure looked more like a leftover from the era of Queen Victoria. Patrick could just imagine all the winding staircases and hidden doors he might find within those walls.

"Interesting," Brooke murmured, then got out of the car.

Every bit as fascinated, Patrick followed and they walked together up the yellow-brick sidewalk that led to the front porch and a massive, stained-glass door.

"I think I'm in love," Brooke murmured, hazel eyes glowing, face flushed. She fairly trembled with excitement, revealing a capacity for passion heretofore unwitnessed and even unsuspected by Patrick.

He recognized that zest for life and living at once since he possessed it himself. And it was through new eyes that he watched Brooke greet the silver-haired woman who answered the door, introduced herself as Dot, and then motioned them to come inside.

"This house is mine and I'm very particular with it," Dot warned as she waddled up the stairs. And waddle, she did, but for all her extra pounds Patrick found her attractive. He suspected she'd been quite a beauty in her youth. A full-length oil portrait on the wall proved he was right.

At the top of the stairs, they turned left, heading down a carpeted hallway until they reached the door at the end of it. Their hostess inserted a key—the kind used to open treasure chests—into the lock and turned it, then pushed open the door.

Brooke, by now so excited she reminded Patrick of his nieces at Christmas, slipped past him and on into the room. She then followed Dot around while Patrick stayed put and listened to her exclamations of pleasure over the ample space, the furniture, the carpeting, the drapes, even the wallpaper.

"How much?" Brooke finally asked her companion when the two of them walked back into the living room.

Dot quoted her a reasonable—shockingly reasonable—monthly rent.

Brooke caught Patrick's eye. He could tell she wondered what was wrong with the apartment to make it so inexpensive. He wondered, too.

"Where's the bathroom?" he asked, certain it must be down the hall.

But Brooke just pointed to a door on the other side of the bedroom.

"Kitchen?"

Brooke pointed again. "And there's a balcony, cable television hook-up, and a telephone jack."

"So what's the catch?" Patrick blurted, unable to contain his curiosity.

"I'm very particular," the owner of the house warned again. "I'll require six local references, two month's rent in advance as a deposit, and a two-year lease."

A two-year lease? Patrick snorted his opinion of that outrageous requirement. No wonder no one wanted to rent the place.

"You can have the two month's rent and the two-year lease," Brooke replied. "But I can't give you six local references."

"How many can you give me?" Dot asked.

"Only three," Brooke said, glancing at Patrick for an okay. He gave it to her with a nod. "I just moved into town."

Dot considered that for a moment. "How many non-local references can you give me?"

"One," Brooke replied. "My employer. That makes four in all. Will you settle for four references, Miss Dot? I promise I'll take good care of your apartment."

Dot clucked her tongue and shook her head, clearly in a quandary. "You'll pay two months' rent in advance?"

"And sign your two-year lease—" Brooke reaffirmed with a nod.

"Are you sure you want to do that?" Patrick interjected, unable to hold his tongue any longer. "Anything could happen in two years. Why, you might meet someone and fall in love. You might decide to get married."

Brooke laughed as though that was the most ridiculous thing anyone had ever said to her.

"All right, then," Patrick said. "You might get tired of living in an apartment and decide to build a house. You never know."

"Oh, yes, I do," Brooke said, then turned to Dot. "So what do you say? Is it a deal?"

"I'll go get the lease," Dot told her, and vanished through the door. A second later, Patrick heard her padding down the stairs.

"I think you're making a big mistake," he said when certain the woman was out of earshot.

"You don't like the apartment?" Brooke asked, frowning.

"I love the apartment. I just—"

"Come here." Brooke beckoned for him to join her by a glass door, then took his hand and led him out onto a balcony. "Is this not the most gorgeous view in all of Amarillo?"

Patrick took note of the skyline, the trees and Miss Dot's rather exquisite poppy bed—California poppies in Texas!—far below. Gorgeous? Yes. But not as gorgeous as the young woman leaning so dangerously far over the rail that bordered the balcony on three sides.

With a sharp intake of breath, he grabbed her dress about waist high and hauled her back to safety.

"Are you trying to kill yourself?" he croaked, capturing her shoulders to give her a little shake much like he'd give Shelly or Emmy in similar circumstances.

But it wasn't a five-year-old girl he held. It was a woman, fully grown and sexy as hell.

She rested her hands on his upper arms, about biceps high, and laughed up at him.

"I feel like celebrating," she exclaimed, eyes sparkling with mischief as she swayed toward him. "Dance with me?"

Dance with me. Dance with me. How many times had Patrick heard those words from Stephanie when she'd dragged him to this or that social function, usually hosted by her well-to-do parents?

Though she knew perfectly well that he'd never learned how, she always asked it of him. And Patrick, blinded by her beauty, always gave her permission to find another partner.

And another... and another... and another.

"I think I'll sit this one out," he growled to Brooke, suddenly reminded that beauty was sometimes only skin deep.

That said, he released her so abruptly she stumbled. He then strode back into the apartment, leaving Brooke alone and feeling foolish for ever having assumed he might want to help her celebrate finding her new home.

Chapter Five

Brooke found the atmosphere in her car downright chilly after she and Patrick got back into it more than an hour later. She glanced at her watch, noting that it was just six o'clock ... early yet.

She still had time to treat Patrick to a burger somewhere—her original plan. But she wasn't sure he'd want to go now.

What had happened on the balcony of her new apartment mere moments ago? What could she have said to so thoroughly destroy five hours of camaraderie?

One minute they stood close, arm-in-arm. The next ...

Brooke sighed softly and risked a sidelong glance at her silent companion. Since he stared out the window, she could not read his expression, but she didn't really need to, after all. In her heart of hearts, she suspected what was wrong, guessed why he'd rebuffed her.

And at once some painful memories resurfaced along with some doubts about herself.

Rejected at age five by her own father, dumped by two boyfriends and a fiancé in later years, Brooke often wondered whether she was unlucky in love or just plain unlovable. She sometimes believed both, a theory Patrick's refusal to dance seemed to reinforce.

Brooke told herself that his brush-off didn't matter, that she'd come to Amarillo to begin again, sans men, anyway.

In reality, however, Patrick's action took its toll on her self-esteem. Brooke Brady asked men to dance as rarely as she gave away hugs and kisses.

And so it was with undeniable disappointment that she abandoned once and for all any thoughts of feeding Patrick, instead speeding back to her motel.

There the two of them exchanged a goodbye so cool that she felt the chill of it the whole time she moved into her apartment and even after she finally crawled between the sheets of her new bed around midnight that night.

The next morning, Monday, Brooke woke up late thanks to her new alarm clock. A quick inspection revealed that she, and not the timepiece, was to blame. All the while muttering her disgust, Brooke showered, dressed, did her hair and face, then dashed downstairs. She saw not another soul as she exited the house, but did note that several cars now littered the gravel parking area out back.

Eastgate Mall, only fifteen minutes from her apartment, bustled with activity—none of it customers, however, since the establishment wouldn't open for business until a week from next Saturday.

Marveling at the number of men still working on the outside of the building, Brooke consulted the layout map her employer had given her, then headed indoors.

More chaos greeted her—chaos in the form of bricklayers, sign painters, window cleaners and who knew what other kind of worker. Wondering how the place would ever be ready in time for a grand opening, Brooke stepped over and around various kinds of clutter, one eye on her map, one on the shops lining the massive walkway.

She saw a music shop, a restaurant, a clothing store. She saw a bookstore, a gift shop and a jeweler's. She also saw a card shop and . . . at last . . . her shoe store.

Oh, the sign wasn't up yet and a security grill hid most of the glass front, but Brooke knew. She knew. And she swelled with pride at the sight.

Her store. Her very own store. Never mind that she'd won it by default and only because the man originally assigned as manager had absconded, leaving the company in a bit of a lurch.

The bottom line was what mattered. The bottom line said Brooke Brady was now in charge of the Ruby's Slipper in Amarillo, Texas, which would be one of the largest in the nation.

Grinning at that accomplishment, she dug her key out of her purse, unlocked the security partition and folded it back into the wall. She then opened the glass door and stepped into her paradise.

Well, not exactly that, she realized a second later, inspecting the clutter of unassembled shelving lying all around. To her left she spied cardboard rolls of what she assumed were signs. To her right, she saw a counter heaped with order books, what looked like unopened mail, and a cash register.

Wow, she thought, at once somewhat daunted. Maybe the Seattle store—the store originally promised to her—would've been a safer bet. It was smaller, established, already in the black.

And a stone's throw from her father, she bitterly reminded herself. Her father and his *family*.

On that thought, Brooke tossed her purse into a corner and began to sort through the mail. She'd made the right decision in taking on this particular store and she knew it.

Given time, she would prove her worth and no runaway managers, Texas twisters or Patrick Sawyers would stop her!

For some time Brooke dealt with the mail, most of it applications from would-be shoe salesmen and women. When she finished with that, she glanced at her watch—a very expensive gold one *mailed* to her by her father upon college graduation—and discovered that it was after ten o'clock.

High time to arrange for installation of a telephone at Ruby's Slipper, she decided. And while she was at that, she would see about activating the jack in her own apartment.

Brooke soon accomplished all those tasks. Since by that time her back ached, her stomach growled, and her legs needed a good stretch, she next opted to take a break.

Without delay, Brooke grabbed her keys and headed out the front door. After locking up, she began a leisurely stroll through the mall. Several people spoke to her. Some even introduced themselves—mostly men— but still a bit depressed about Patrick's rejection, Brooke paid no heed to the phenomenon.

Instead she walked up and down each corridor, grateful for the exercise that eased the cramp in her neck. After making a complete loop through the massive structure, she wound up in her own wing and began an inspection of the businesses closest to her.

She saw an ice cream parlor, a dress shop, and, right next door, a video arcade.

Great, Brooke thought without enthusiasm as she eyed the portals of The Electric Rainbow. For a moment the significance of the arcade's name escaped her, then she recalled her one and only memorable visit to such an establishment. All of the machines were electric, she realized. And quite colorful, too.

They were also loud. Very loud.

She frowned, thinking of the bings, bongs, zaps, jing-a-lings and cha-chings that emanated from most video games. Such sounds would get old fast, she knew, and was not thrilled that she would be hearing them from nine to nine, six days of the week, and one to six on Sundays.

"So what do you think of The Electric Rainbow?"

Brooke jumped at the sound of a male voice—a familiar voice—right behind her. She turned and was pleasantly surprised to see that Patrick, who'd said he owned a business somewhere in this mall, had slipped up on her again and now stood nearby.

"I think another name would be more appropriate," Brooke grumbled, deliberately shifting her gaze from the delectable height and breadth of him to the video arcade. "Like maybe Electric Nuisance."

He stood in silence for a moment, digesting that comment. "And why is that?"

"Arcades are noisy and usually infested by rowdy teenagers who litter, that's why." She sighed her disgust. "I wonder why Ralph Lloyd selected this location for Ruby's Slipper? You'd think he'd have more sense than to settle next door to an arcade. Or maybe it wasn't there when he chose this particular spot...."

"For your information," Patrick said rather coolly, "The Electric Rainbow was the very first business to rent space in this mall."

"Oh?" Brooke wondered at his knowledge *and* at his tone. He actually sounded miffed.

"Yes, and the promoters were very pleased to have me aboard."

Oops. "To...have...*you* aboard?"

"To have me aboard," he repeated. "They were familiar with my reputation as a sound businessman. They knew I'd pay my rent on time and honor my lease."

"I see." And she did—dark eyes that flashed with anger, cheeks flushed crimson with agitation. "Patrick, I—"

"You needn't worry about the noise. The walls are doubly insulated and I'll be sure to keep the doors closed. As for the rowdy teenagers...I run a tight ship. No one from my place is going to bother you."

Oh, dear. "I—I didn't know you were the owner of this arcade," Brooke blurted, laying a hand on his arm.

"And if you had?"

"I wouldn't have said anything," Brooke assured him.

"But you'd still have thought it?"

"Well...yes. Probably. But that's only because—" Abruptly, Brooke halted her explanation. She really didn't owe this man any sort of explanation for her opinion. And there was no one there to hear it now, anyway. Patrick had vanished into his place of business.

Still tempted to follow and explain why she harbored such prejudice against video arcades, Brooke did not. Why should she crawl after Patrick every time he lost his temper, which was way too much?

Because it's usually your fault.

"It is not," Brooke murmured aloud to her conscience. Then, huffing her exasperation, she unlocked her front door, swept through it and tackled, with energy born of frustration, what had to be done.

Hours later, Brooke dragged her weary body up the staircase at Dot's Victorian mansion. This time, she saw a man and a woman sitting in the spacious, plant-adorned foyer. They acknowledged her with curious nods, but Brooke didn't linger long enough to introduce herself.

She simply didn't have the energy at the moment.

Once inside the apartment, she tossed down her purse and made a beeline to the phone jack, into which she plugged the telephone she'd picked up at a discount store on the way home.

After testing it by dialing a weather information service, she plopped face down across the bed and didn't move a muscle for a good thirty minutes except to cover her head with a pillow.

Unfortunately her brain could not be as still, and Brooke found herself rehashing the events of the day, in particular, her run-in with Patrick. In retrospect, she realized she should never have voiced her opinion.

So what now? she wondered.

Apologize?

That seemed appropriate, for sure. And easy enough to accomplish since she would probably see him around the mall.

If he didn't avoid her, that is.

If he *did* . . .

Somewhere a phone rang. Drowsy and safe under her feather pillow, Brooke ignored it for the first three rings. Then, with a gasp of remembrance, she tossed the pillow aside and lunged for her new telephone, sitting on the table next to her four-poster.

"Hello?"

"Brooke? It's Sarah. I called Information for your number. I hope you don't mind."

"Of course not," Brooke replied. "I'm amazed they had it already. I just plugged in the phone five minutes ago."

Sarah laughed. "Mindboggling, isn't it?"

Brooke could only agree.

"The reason I called is that I was wondering if you really meant it when you said you'd help me with my algebra."

"I meant it," Brooke replied, tactfully not verbalizing the *please not tonight* that hovered on the tip of her tongue.

"Oh, good." Sarah's relief came across the line loud and clear. "Are you available tonight? I have a test tomorrow and I'm just not ready for it."

Brooke's shoulders sagged. "Tonight, you say?"

"Yes. I wasn't going to call, knowing how hard you must have worked today. But then I thought you might just be willing to swap a home-cooked meal for a little knowledge, especially if I promised not to keep you too late."

"Home-cooked meal, huh?"

"That's right. Fried chicken, mashed potatoes, gravy, green beans, biscuits...."

Brooke sighed. "What time do you want me?"

"When can you get here?"

"In an hour?"

"I'll have the food on the table."

True to her word, Sarah motioned Brooke right to the table when she arrived at Patrick's house. There she ate until she could hold no more, along with Sarah, Emmy and Shelly, who reported on the whereabouts of their Great Uncle Gil—a movie with a lady friend—Cynthia—a baby shower—and Patrick—up in his office.

The twins expressed wonder that their uncle wasn't downstairs stuffing himself with fried chicken, his favorite meal, according to them.

Brooke, however, wasn't a bit surprised and figured he'd probably made his decision to skip the meal when he found out she'd be sitting at his table.

"That sure isn't like him," Sarah murmured, words that reinforced Brooke's assumption.

"It's my fault," she therefore admitted. "I hurt his feelings today." With as few words as possible, Brooke explained her faux pas. "Obviously he can't bear the sight of me. Why else would he miss his favorite meal?"

Instead of answering right away, Sarah nodded to excuse her too interested granddaughters from the table. Grumbling, they headed into the den, from where the television blared a second later.

"I think you're wrong about Patrick," Sarah told Brooke once they were alone. "I believe that his hiding upstairs proves something altogether different."

Brooke arched an eyebrow. "And what's that?"

"He doesn't dislike you at all. He likes you."

Brooke laughed aloud at that ridiculous statement. "That doesn't make sense."

"Sure it does," Sarah replied, rising to gather up dirty plates. "If he didn't like you, he wouldn't care what you think or do. And if he didn't care what you think or do, he wouldn't turn down my fried chicken just because you happen to be here eating it, too."

Brooke thought about that for a moment, then shook her head and stood to help her hostess clear the table. "That won't wash. What if he doesn't care what I think or do, but still won't eat because he couldn't enjoy his meal with me anywhere around?"

"Poppycock!" Sarah headed to the kitchen with her load, Brooke one step behind. "He's avoiding you because he likes you so much he's afraid he'll love you. And Patrick hasn't had much luck with love."

Love? Every hair on Brooke's head stood on end at the mere mention of the word—probably because she hadn't had much luck with it, either.

"Trust me," Sarah continued. "A mother knows." That said, she motioned Brooke back into the den. "I'm leaving these dishes for later. Now we'd better get to work on this algebra. I've got to make at least a B on this test tomorrow to maintain my grade point average."

Though Brooke's head positively spun with crazy conjectures and unanswered questions, she sat down beside Sarah and somehow gave the woman her attention. They worked nonstop until nine, at which point Cynthia returned complaining of a "terrible" headache, then until ten, when Gilbert wheeled himself in.

At that point, Sarah pronounced herself an "expert" and instructed Brooke to reward herself with a slice of pecan pie, stashed in the refrigerator. The woman then headed in the other direction to check on Cynthia.

Grateful to end the lesson, hungry for the pie, Brooke walked to the kitchen swing door and gave it a firm push...right into Patrick's backside. He yelped when it hit him and jostled the glass of milk he held— milk that sloshed out onto Sarah's shiny linoleum floor.

"I'm so sorry," Brooke exclaimed, slipping into the room. She hurried to the sink for a dishcloth, only to run into Patrick again since he naturally moved in the same direction.

"You stay put," he gruffly ordered, depositing his milk glass on the counter next to a plate heaped with leftover chicken and biscuits.

"I was only trying to help," Brooke told him as he moved away. Then she sighed. "Why is it that no matter what I say or do around this man it's always wrong?"

Her words, though spoken more to herself than to Patrick, stopped him dead in his tracks. He pivoted to face her. "Is that what you think?"

"That's what I *know.*"

"You're wrong," he said, words that astonished her.

"Then why are you always angry with me?" Brooke demanded.

"I'm not."

"Yes, you are," she argued. "Why, just look at you now—your face is flushed, your hands are shaking, and your eyes..." To her astonishment, Brooke found herself looking right into those dark eyes, which glowed as expected, but not with anger. No, not with anger at all. "Your eyes..."

"What about them?" Patrick asked, stepping even closer. Brooke took a matching step back and suddenly found her tush pressed against a counter.

"They're just gorgeous. In fact, I believe you have the longest, thickest eyelashes I ever saw on a man."

"And that means I'm angry at you?"

"Oh, n-no, of course not," Brooke stammered, even as Patrick took another step forward. Since she had no place to go, only inches separated them now. Her gaze leveled to his lips. And with a bone-jarring shock, Brooke—the woman who avoided physical contact—realized she wanted to kiss Patrick Sawyer. "That proves...I mean...oh, who cares!" she blurted, throwing her arms around his neck and giving in to impulse.

Here are your BIG WIN Game Tickets potentially worth from $100.00 to $1,000,000.00 each. Scratch off the PINK METALLIC STRIP on each of your Sweepstakes tickets to see what you could win and mail your entry right away. (SEE OFFICIAL RULES IN BACK OF BOOK FOR DETAILS!)

This could be your lucky day – GOOD LUCK!

TICKET 1
Scratch PINK METALLIC STRIP to reveal potential value of this ticket if it is a winning ticket. Return all game tickets intact.

LUCKY NUMBER

1L 524114

TICKET 2
Scratch PINK METALLIC STRIP to reveal potential value of this ticket if it is a winning ticket. Return all game tickets intact.

LUCKY NUMBER

4U 631711

TICKET 3
Scratch PINK METALLIC STRIP to reveal potential value of this ticket if it is a winning ticket. Return all game tickets intact.

LUCKY NUMBER

3M 511889

TICKET 4
Scratch PINK METALLIC STRIP to reveal potential value of this ticket if it is a winning ticket. Return all game tickets intact.

LUCKY NUMBER

9P 517562

TICKET 5
We're giving away brand new books to selected individuals. Scratch PINK METALLIC STRIP for number of free books you will receive.

AUTHORIZATION CODE

130107-742

TICKET 6
We have an outstanding added gift for you if you are accepting our free books. Scratch PINK METALLIC STRIP to reveal gift.

AUTHORIZATION CODE

130107-742

YES! Enter my Lucky Numbers in THE BIG WIN Sweepstakes and when winners are selected, tell me if I've won any prize. If the PINK METALLIC STRIP is scratched off on ticket #5, I will also receive one or more FREE Silhouette Romance™ novels along with the FREE GIFT on ticket #6, as explained on the back and on the opposite page.

215 CIS AH75 (U-SIL-R-06/93)

NAME _____

ADDRESS _____ APT. _____

CITY _____ STATE _____ ZIP CODE _____

THE SILHOUETTE READER SERVICE™: HERE'S HOW IT WORKS

Accepting free books puts you under no obligation to buy anything. You may keep the books and gift and return the shipping statement marked ''cancel.'' If you do not cancel, about a month later we will send you 6 additional novels, and bill you just $1.99 each plus 25¢ delivery and applicable sales tax, if any.* That's the complete price, and—compared to cover prices of $2.75 each—quite a bargain! You may cancel at any time, but if you choose to continue, every month we'll send you 6 more books, which you may either purchase at the discount price . . . or return at our expense and cancel your subscription.

* Terms and prices subject to change without notice. Sales tax applicable in N.Y.

BUSINESS REPLY MAIL

FIRST CLASS MAIL   PERMIT NO. 717   BUFFALO, NY

POSTAGE WILL BE PAID BY ADDRESSEE

SILHOUETTE READER SERVICE
3010 WALDEN AVE
PO BOX 1867
BUFFALO NY 14240-9952

NO POSTAGE
NECESSARY
IF MAILED
IN THE
UNITED STATES

On a scale of one to ten, the kiss rated barely a six ... until Patrick recovered from the shock. Then it earned a whopping perfect score.

Brooke found herself tugged forward into his embrace and up on her tingling toes before he lifted her to where she sat perched on the edge of the counter. That move put them heart to heart, and Brooke's hammered like crazy against his.

At once breathless from the crushing contact, she ended the kiss and tipped her head back, baring her neck to Patrick. He immediately touched his lips to the sensitive flesh just under her ear, then nibbled his way across her cheek to her mouth so he could kiss her again.

Lost to the magic of his touch, Brooke savored each and every sensation. She relished the taste of him, inhaled his scent, heard his ragged breaths. She opened her eyes and found him watching her, then shivered when he traced a path down her spine with his fingers.

Clearly encouraged by her response, Patrick cupped her hips in his hands to hold her firmly in place while he maneuvered his way between her knees and pressed his lower body closer.

"Ah, Brooke," he breathed between kisses planted on her chin, eyes and nose. "I—"

A sudden crashing sound made both of them jump.

In one dizzying instant Brooke found herself abandoned there on the counter. She hopped right to the floor to keep from falling on her face, then and only then registering the fact that she and Patrick were no longer alone.

Emmy and Shelly stood just inside the swing door, dressed in identically designed summer gowns, one baby blue, one mint green. Had they seen anything? Brooke instantly wondered.

"Hiya, girls," Patrick drawled as he scooped up his plate and drink. "Looking for a midnight snack, too?"

"We're looking for *you*," Emmy told him, her accusing gaze first on him, then on Brooke. "We didn't get our story tonight."

"No story," Shelly agreed. The twins then exchanged a long look, after which Shelly whispered something to Emmy that made them both giggle.

Brooke felt Patrick's gaze on her. Raising her own to meet his, she exchanged an equally long look with him, but neither laughed.

"It's rude to whisper, Michele," he said instead, turning to face his niece. "Want to tell us the secret?"

Shelly hesitated, then shook her head.

Patrick directed his attention to his other niece. "Emmaline?"

"She said 'I told you boys and girls are supposed to kiss on the mouth.' "

"I see," murmured Patrick.

And so, Brooke realized, had the twins—too darn much. Blushing furiously, she began to ease toward the door. Patrick, now walking over to the dinette set situated in one corner of the room, didn't appear to notice. He sat down, seemingly unperturbed, and took a drink of milk.

"Sure y'all don't want something to eat? I'll share."

The girls exchanged another look, then hustled over to join him at the table, beruffled gowns flapping around their legs with every step. Torn between escape and watching Patrick in action, Brooke leaned lightly against the swing door but made no move to slip through it just yet.

"I guess you two saw me and Brooke kissing a while ago, huh?" Patrick commented once he'd handed each girl a chicken leg and a napkin.

Both nodded.

"Is there anything either of you wants to ask about it?"

Emmy and Shelly considered that quite seriously for a moment, then Shelly nodded again.

"Is Brooke going to have a baby now?" she asked, a question that propelled Brooke out the door and to her car... at a dead run.

Chapter Six

The moment Patrick arrived at Eastgate Mall Tuesday afternoon, he headed straight to Ruby's Slipper. Brooke, seated on the floor at the back of the store, looked up when the security bells announced his entry, and then blushed scarlet upon recognizing who'd come to call.

Patrick wasn't a bit surprised by her reaction. He'd be embarrassed, too, if he'd acted the coward as she had the night before.

And what a night—hot kisses, wide-eyed nieces, bribes, and sweet, sweet dreams.

"Hi, there," Brooke said, flashing that smile of hers.

Refusing to be charmed by it today, Patrick walked right over to the floor where she sat, surrounded by metal shelving, screws, and an electric screwdriver. He crossed his arms over his chest and looked down at her, his expression as stern as he could make it considering she looked all of eighteen, sitting there like that, and innocent as a babe.

"Don't 'hi' me," he told her. "What do you mean running off like that last night, leaving me to face the music alone?"

To his astonishment, Brooke bubbled with laughter—a delightful sound that warmed his heart and melted what little remained of his temper.

"I'm sorry," she told him, and wiped at a tear snaking down her cheek. "But you were doing so well . . ."

"'Well' hell," he exclaimed, a reply that resulted in more laughter from his companion. Patrick stole a moment to check out her hairdo—loose and curled—and her clothes—navy pants and a bright green blouse. Silently approving them all, he added, "I'll have you know I had to bribe those little shysters."

"Yeah? With what?"

"A trip to the park on Saturday. And guess who's coming with us . . ." He glared at her with mock ferocity.

"Don't look at me," she retorted, getting to her feet, and brushing off her cute little fanny. "I have too much work to do to gallivant around the park with *your* nieces."

"What kind of work?" Patrick asked.

"This," Brooke told him, pointing to material lying at her feet. "I've been fiddling with this darn shelving all morning, and I don't have one completed yet. I need help.''

"Let me take a look," Patrick said, instantly intrigued.

Brooke brushed her hair back out of her face, then reached for what turned out to be assembly instructions written in four languages and, as far as she could tell, not decipherable in any of them.

"Good luck," Brooke murmured as she passed them over to him. "You'll need it."

With a preoccupied grunt, Patrick began to study the instructions. He scanned what lay strewn all about, took note of her tools, then nodded.

"All right, here's the plan," he announced. "I put the shelving together. You spend Saturday in the park with Emmy, Shelly, and me."

Brooke never blinked an eye. "You've got a deal."

"Not so fast," he said, holding up a hand to caution her. "This looks like a lot of work, and since you're partly to blame for my having to cater to the twins on Saturday, there's one more condition to this little bargain."

"Oh? And what's that?" She looked so suspicious Patrick wondered if she could read minds.

"I get a kiss for every shelf I put together."

Instead of slapping his face, the response he expected to his impulsive, outrageous, totally bizarre suggestion, Brooke actually seemed to consider it quite seriously.

"Each shelf or each unit?" she asked.

"Each shelf." Crazy, Patrick might be, but never a fool.

"That's—" she paused to figure up; her eyes rounded "—eighty kisses!"

Patrick nodded. "And five are payable in advance."

"You're out of your mind."

Almost certainly, he silently agreed, since he could think of no other excuse for his behavior. Who'd believe that mere days ago he was satisfied with his safe, solitary existence?

Satisfied? Certainly. Happy? Not exactly. But he never had to worry about what some woman might be plotting.

As for this particular one, Patrick didn't need to read her mind to know she would never go for his bargain. And that was just as well. He never should have made it in the first place....

"But I'm out of mine, too," Brooke continued, jerking him back to the present. "So I agree to your terms. When do you want the down payment?"

"Now."

"Here?" she asked, indicating the store with its plate-glass front through which any number of workers could witness his demise.

"No, here," he teased, suddenly lighthearted, and pointing to his mouth.

Brooke just sighed and took his hand. She led him to a small, poorly illuminated stockroom, backed him to the wall and then, before he could get his bearings, brushed her lips over his in the briefest of kisses.

"You call that a kiss?" Patrick demanded, even though his heart pumped double-time.

"I get better with practice," she promised, then proceeded to prove her theory.

She kissed him hard. She kissed him long. She kissed him out of his mind . . . three times.

Thankful for the wall that held him up, Patrick cherished each and every one of those kisses and returned them with admirable enthusiasm. He was rewarded for his efforts with Brooke's sighs and moans, little sounds that turned him inside out and made him wish he could give her more than just kisses.

"This is the last one, " Brooke warned rather breathlessly when they pulled apart that fourth time.

"Let's make it special," Patrick murmured, sliding his hands up over her back and then under her arms to cup her breasts. She tensed ever so slightly, but said nothing . . . even when his thumbs teased the peaks to pebble hardness through her blouse.

Ever careful of her desires, his eyes locked with hers, Patrick slowly unbuttoned one button and then another of her blouse until he could push the silky fabric aside. With his finger he traced the swell of each breast, right where it vanished into her lacy bra.

Once again, Brooke tensed, and taking that as an *I'm not so sure about this,* Patrick kissed the pulse in her throat, then pulled the blouse back together. "One more kiss, you say?"

She nodded rather tremulously.

Tipping his head forward, Patrick gave her that kiss, to which she responded with an abandon that

made him wonder just how far she would have gone
with him here in this dusty old stockroom.

He teased her lips with his tongue, then probed the
recesses of her mouth when she allowed him entry. He
savored the taste of her—felt immediate loss when she
finally pulled away from him and lowered her heels.

"That's the five," she said, her voice husky-soft and
warm.

"Yeah."

"Sure that's enough?"

Hot damn. "Well, sixteen might be more realistic.
That would be, um, twenty percent of the total debt—
a common down payment."

"Sixteen? Hmm..." she murmured, swaying forward, raising her heels until their mouths could meet.

At that instant Patrick heard bells...the security
bells on the front door.

"Are you expecting anyone?" he asked Brooke.

She started to shake her head, then gasped. "Is it
one o'clock?"

Patrick peered at his watch and nodded.

"Then, yes, I'm expecting someone. My applicants. Oh my gosh..." She whirled and managed two
steps toward the door before Patrick caught up with
her.

"Button up," Patrick brusquely ordered, sweeping
past to exit the stockroom. In the store proper, he
smoothly greeted the young woman who stood near
the door, eyeing the premises with some curiosity.
"Are you here for an interview?"

"Yes," she told him.

"Good. Miss Brady will be right out." That said, he got to the business at hand—assembling shelving.

What else could he do, having already received such a hefty down payment on services rendered?

"Well, that's one I can't hire," Brooke murmured in utter disgust when the young woman left the store some twenty minutes later.

"Why not?" Patrick asked from where he now sat on the floor. "She seemed very knowledgeable."

"Too knowledgeable, actually, at least about us. You have lipstick all over your shirt, Patrick Sawyer. Lipstick that's the same color as what I'm wearing. She'd have to be blind to miss it."

He glance down, hooting with laughter when he confirmed her statement. "So I have. So I have."

"Do you, by any chance, have another shirt?" Brooke asked.

"In my car."

"Would you please go get it? I have three more applicants coming this afternoon, the next in about five minutes. We're going to be the talk of the mall if we're not careful."

Patrick grinned. "Would that be so bad?"

"Yes," Brooke replied, and meant it. The very last thing she needed in her new life was scandal.

And the second to last was a man, she acknowledged as Patrick got to his feet with a groan and headed obediently out the door.

Thankfully alone, Brooke relived their idle in the stockroom. She recalled her wanton behavior, cringing when she realized how close she'd come to making love with Patrick right there.

Worse, she'd really wanted to . . . a first for Brooke. The touch of his hands on her breasts had excited her more than she'd ever imagined possible. And the intensity of that response scared her half to death, almost as much as the realization that Patrick obviously didn't find her so unlovable as she'd imagined.

Un-love-a-ble. Brooke dissected that four-syllable word and focused in on the second syllable: love.

She pronounced the word aloud. "Love." And her voice echoed in the empty room.

An interesting concept, love, she decided, and one that had nothing whatsoever to do with what had just transpired in the stockroom.

That was *sex*. No-strings fun and games born of mutual attraction.

Temptation.

And what did a single woman, trying to make a new home for herself, need with such temptation? Heaven knew she had enough to worry about without *that*.

So what now? she asked herself, instantly depressed at the thought of never kissing Patrick again.

Now? Hard work and dedication.

Later? Maybe an affair. Maybe.

But is that what she really wanted? An affair? Brooke didn't even have to think about that question. As millions of other romantic hopefuls on the planet, she wanted love. And with it, all the trimmings: a wedding, a mortgage, children. . . .

"You fool," she murmured, amazed at her own die-hard optimism. If her own father couldn't love her, what made her think any other man could?

Patrick didn't finish the shelves that evening, though he did manage to assemble all but one unit.

Why he didn't complete it—he had time—Patrick didn't really know. He had a good idea, though: second thoughts. If he didn't have to finish the shelves, he wouldn't have to collect the bounty owed him.

Not that Patrick hadn't enjoyed those heart-stopping kisses back there in the stockroom. He had. Too much.

Way too much.

And now a bit worried that he might develop an insatiable craving for the same, Patrick hesitated to tempt fate by indulging himself in another seventy-five of them.

For that reason, he held off on completion of the shelves. And for that reason, he didn't hang around and wait for her to finish her last interview. He didn't trust himself not to ask her to dinner, drive her to her new apartment, try out her new bed.

As if she'd let him.

Would she let me?

Patrick wondered about that all the way home and far into the night. On the one hand, he found himself intrigued by the possibility that a woman so reserved as Brooke—and she was reserved, stockroom kisses or no—could become involved with him on a sexual level.

On the other hand, he worried that his own participation in such an affair might be more than physical. He cared for her already, after all. She could easily get under his skin—just like Stephanie—and play him for a fool.

And having once played the part, Patrick didn't want to do it again.

So what now? he asked himself upon rising Wednesday morning. Do I finish those shelves today, play with fire by collecting those sizzling kisses?

Or do I find some other work to do? Make my excuses? Turn tail and run?

Heaven knew Patrick had plenty of other things to keep him occupied. Between rebuilding his car wash—which had been fully insured and was now minus the red convertible—and the grand opening of The Electric Rainbow, he wouldn't have to lie to Brooke.

He could keep his distance until Saturday, at which time he'd see her again with the twins, perfect chaperons, in tow. The relief that washed over Patrick on that thought told him he wasn't near ready for seventy-five kisses from Brooke.

For that reason, he did little more than stick his head in the door of Ruby's Slipper, beg a raincheck on his little project, and then escape to his own place of business.

He did the same on Thursday, only to discover that she had finished up the shelves herself.

"You're just as busy as I am," she told him, making no mention of kisses owed.

Patrick didn't mention them, either, and paid for his reticence the whole rest of the day by wondering if she'd found them forgettable or dangerous.

He hoped dangerous, which reinforced the wisdom of his delaying tactics of the past two days.

If she found the kisses dangerous, and he did, too, then they were both in a whole lot of trouble.

On Friday, Brooke found herself casting longing glances toward the door of Ruby's Slipper all morning. Would Patrick come by the shoe store today to collect his kisses?

And if he did, would she give them to him?

At noon, when Patrick still hadn't shown, Brooke accepted the truth she suspected the first time he'd made excuses to her. Patrick no longer wanted the kisses she owed him. And though vastly relieved that she would not be subjected to such temptation, Brooke couldn't help but wonder just why he'd changed his mind.

She also wondered about Saturday. Did he still want her to accompany him and his nieces to the park? Other than mentioning such an excursion that one time, he hadn't brought it up again. She didn't know what to wear, how to get there, or what time they intended to go.

That was why, with a sigh of pure exasperation, Brooke grabbed her purse, exited the shop and locked the door just minutes after twelve o'clock. She headed next door immediately, fully intending to confront Patrick, only to find the place locked up tight.

No wonder he hadn't dropped in today. He wasn't even in the mall.

Did that mean he would've if he could've?

"Brooke Brady, get a grip!" she scolded aloud, an order that raised more than one appreciative construction worker's eyebrow.

But she never noticed. Instead she headed right for her car and then the nearest pizza parlor, where she indulged herself in a meal from the buffet, the best cure yet for a terminal case of confusion.

Brooke worked hard all the rest of the afternoon, so hard that she nearly jumped out of her skin when the security bells on her door chimed.

"Would you look at this?" Patrick exclaimed as he walked into her store, all smiles, and looking as if he didn't have a worry in the world. "You've worked a miracle, Brooke. You really have."

Although a little leery of him, Brooke appreciated the compliment and glanced around trying to see the neat rows of shelving, the signs, and the spotless countertop through someone else's eyes.

It did look good, she decided. "Thanks. I've worked hard this week and that means a lot to me."

"So hard that you can take off tomorrow, right?"

So they were still on! Brooke could have kicked herself, so disgusted was she by the joy that welled within her.

"I don't know," she replied very casually. "I have an awful lot of Saturday things to do."

"Such as?" He stood right across the counter from her now and so close she could smell his after-shave again. That smell, spicy and sexy as before, transported her instantly to another time, as scents often do, and Brooke found her thoughts back in the stockroom, her gaze on Patrick's mouth.

"Um . . ." What were they talking about?

"Brooke?"

"Oh, um, groceries. I have to get groceries. I've eaten out all week because I haven't had time to do that yet. I also have some laundry to do, some personal bills to pay, and I have to buy myself a television. My apartment is just too quiet."

"Are you saying you can't come with us to the park?"

Here's your chance, Brooke! Get out of it. "I'm saying I can't stay there all day."

"Then there's no problem," Patrick said. "I'll pick you up at nine and have you home by one o'clock— two at the latest."

"I guess that'll be all right," Brooke replied with some hesitancy, immediately wishing she'd listened to her brain and not her loudmouthed heart.

Patrick left shortly after and without so much as a mention of the kisses that she owed him. As relieved as she was disappointed, Brooke turned her attention to the telephone. She spent the next half hour hiring part-time clerks, both female, and arranging their work schedules. She then focused her energies on setting up the books, paying bills, and all the other duties that naturally fell to the manager of a store this large.

Brooke left that afternoon feeling quite proud of all she'd accomplished during her first five days on the job. And though she knew she could find plenty to do if she worked on Saturday, she also knew it was time for a break. More than one manager had overextended themselves at this point in their career. Having been forewarned during training about the toll such folly could take, Brooke didn't intend to let that happen to her.

Saturday dawned bright and clear. Brooke opened her eyes when a stray sunbeam landed on them, stretched lazily, and then just lay in bed cherishing the fact that she didn't have to drag herself out of bed and rush to the mall.

She scanned the room, making the most of this opportunity to study every nook and cranny, something she hadn't really had time to do all week. The grace and beauty of her apartment charmed her, but it lacked the personal touches that could turn this house into the home she sought.

Since all the things that would have lent such a touch had been lost to the tornado, Brooke vowed to do a little shopping around once she got free of Patrick and his charges. An antique enthusiast, she liked the idea of surrounding herself with knickknacks, vases and even furniture once owned and loved by someone else.

There was nothing, Brooke thought, quite as much fun as trying to guess what occasion might have prompted the giving of a certain elegant urn or maybe a piece of fine jewelry. She imagined the love of the giver, the joy of the recipient, and borrowed those emotions, making them her own.

Secondhand happiness.

All she'd ever really known.

"Oh, get a life!" Brooke exclaimed, suddenly impatient with her maudlin thoughts. She threw back the covers and bounced out of bed, fully determined to do just that.

Brooke washed her hair, then French braided it down the back again, before choosing what to wear. Since she didn't have much in the way of casual apparel, the choice was an easy one—red T-shirt, white pants and strappy sandals.

Breakfast consisted of cinnamon toast, made in the oven. Brooke added *toaster* to her ongoing list of needs, then carried her toast and a glass of orange juice out to her balcony, where she ate it.

A slight breeze blew, rustling the leaves of the tall oak right next to the house. Below, Brooke spied Dot at work in her beautiful red poppy bed.

An interesting person, Dot, she decided, promising herself she would get to know the woman better as soon as she had time. Grand opening would be over in a matter of days, after all, and she had signed a two-year lease.

Thoughts of that lease reminded Brooke of Patrick's warnings about falling in love and marrying.

Could that happen? she found herself wondering. Could she ever believe in herself enough to trust any man's vow of lifetime devotion?

The sound of crunching gravel drew Brooke's gaze to the driveway just as Sarah's minivan rolled to a stop. From it sprang Emmy and Shelly, who darted for the house, Patrick hurrying behind.

"Wait up, girls!" Brooke heard him call. And since those three words rang with frustration, she deposited her glass in the sink, grabbed her purse and headed out the door to greet them.

Seconds later found the four of them on their way to the park.

Brooke loved the place on sight. Shady, cool, with a running trail, Junglegym, swings and an old metal merry-go-round, it called to the little girl in her. For that reason, she almost wished she was five years old again, like Emmy and Shelly.

But five wasn't a good year for her, and not for anything would Brooke have relived the death of her mother or the retreat of her father.

"Why don't we sit right here and let the girls have at it?" Patrick said, pointing to a park bench near a shallow creek.

Brooke nodded and followed him to the bench, then sat primly at one end after he sat at the other. To her amazement, Emmy and Shelly wedged between them instead of going to play.

"What are you two doing?" Patrick demanded, clearly as surprised as Brooke.

The girls exchanged a rather guilty look.

"Vis'ting."

"Visiting, huh?" Patrick shook his head and sighed. "Okay. Let's visit. How are you ladies today?"

Emmy giggled. "Fine."

"And what about you, Miss Michele?" he then asked.

"Fine."

"You both look mighty pretty," Patrick said next, eyeing Shelly's green short set and Emmy's blue one. "New outfits?"

Both girls nodded.

"Did your mom make them?"

Shelly giggled. "You know she didn't."

"So where did they come from?"

"You bought them for us at Wal-Mart, silly."

"So you think I'm silly?" Patrick asked.

"Uh-huh," his nieces chorused.

"Well that makes three sillies sitting on this old bench," Patrick told them.

"Me n' Shelly are not either silly," Emmy argued.

"What else do you call sitting here when there are swings *right over there?*"

To Brooke's amusement, the girls exchanged another look, then bounded off the bench and over to the swings.

"Very clever," she commented to Patrick the moment they were alone.

"I do have my moments," he smoothly acknowledged ... words with which Brooke could only agree.

Chapter Seven

Unfortunately, this particular moment didn't produce lasting results. In ten minutes the girls were back on the bench, again watching Brooke and Patrick with solemn blue eyes.

"Are you done already?" he asked, more than a little frustrated by their behavior. Usually he couldn't keep up with them. Today, they stuck to him like glue.

Both nodded.

"So go play on the merry-go-round." He pointed to it just in case they didn't know the way.

"We'd rather stay here," Shelly replied, and settled herself more comfortably on the bench.

"Why, for Pete's sake?" Patrick demanded, at the end of his rope.

"Who's Pete?"

"Why, dammit?"

"'Cause we don't want to miss no kisses," blurted Emmy, eyeing him with some alarm.

"Any kisses. *Any* kisses," Patrick corrected automatically as he fumbled through his brain for a way out of this one. He decided that honesty might be his best bet, and so gave it a shot. "Brooke and I aren't going to kiss today. You two won't miss anything if you go play."

"Promise?" This from Shelly, who looked darned doubtful.

"I promise."

The girls considered his reply, conferred in whispers, and hopped off the bench. Without another word, they headed for the merry-go-round, which soon spun to the accompaniment of their squeals and giggles.

"Sorry about that," Patrick murmured, highly aware of his companion sitting so silent on her end of the too long bench.

"That's okay," she replied, adding, "It was a logical assumption for five-year-olds to make."

"Yeah," he smoothly agreed, raising his gaze to hers. "How would they know that stolen kisses seldom mean anything?"

"Yeah." She laughed softly, from all appearances truly amused by the antics of his nieces.

Patrick's heart sank at the sound, and he realized he'd wished for another reaction...like maybe disappointment or an argument.

Heaven knew *he'd* experienced a letdown, what with his nieces being so observant and Brooke being so distant. Never mind that he'd once thought it would be smart to have Emmy and Shelly along to chaperon. Now that he'd laid eyes on Brooke—beautiful Brooke—again, he wished they were alone so he could present her with a bill for those seventy-five kisses she owed.

Something of his lustful thoughts must have transmitted itself to Brooke. For she suddenly blushed quite charmingly and turned her head to stare at, of all things, a trash barrel.

Pleased that she hadn't slapped his face, instead, Patrick came to a sudden decision.

"About those kisses you owe me . . ."

She tensed and shifted her gaze to him.

"I was thinking about a time-pay plan. I figured that might be, um, safer than your paying them all at once . . ."

"Safer?" She looked right into his eyes, and his heart ker-thunked in response.

"Infinitely."

"Hmm," Brooke murmured, making a great show of considering his suggestion. Her eyes twinkled, a phenomenon Patrick found as charming as her blush. "So how many would you want at a time? How many would you consider . . . *safe?*"

Patrick, at once on fire for her, nearly choked, knowing one might be enough to send him over the edge of control. "How many did you pay down?" As if he didn't know.

"Five, wasn't it?" As if *she* didn't.

"Five. Yeah." He swallowed hard. "Since we both survived those okay—" *Liar!* "—why don't we just proceed five at a time?"

"Okay. Beginning when?"

"Now."

"But you promised the twins..."

"Damn." He sucked in a shaky breath. "Okay. I've got it. We'll begin tonight... after I dump the girls."

"For shame!" Brooke scolded, laughing.

"Sorry," Patrick muttered, but not from the heart.

Brooke thought the day would never end. Not that she didn't have fun. She did, and found the break from work rejuvenating. But five hours of two five-year-olds proved too trying.

The twins were not pleased that Patrick drove them all the way to Emerald City *before* he took Brooke to her apartment. They fussed, they fumed, they argued, but Patrick stood firm and deposited them on his doorstep without ceremony promptly at two o'clock.

Brooke's stomach knotted the moment he slipped back behind the wheel of the minivan. Why, she couldn't be sure, but guessed it had lots to do with the possessive gleam in his gorgeous brown eyes.

"Where to?" he asked, a question that surprised her.

"My apartment, I guess."

"Don't you have to buy a television?"

"Well, yes, but—"

"Then where to?"

Brooke hesitated only a second before answering, "Someplace cheap. I'm simply trying to get by for now."

"I know just the place," Patrick murmured, putting the vehicle in gear. He backed into the street, shifted into Drive, drove until the house disappeared from view, then braked so sharply Brooke found herself thrown against the seat belt.

Patrick gave no explanation, just unsnapped his own seat belt and leaned over to give her a big kiss right on her unsuspecting mouth. Only then did he speak.

"Couldn't wait another minute."

"Oh," she breathed.

"We'll take care of the other four later... at your place."

"Oh!"

Silence reigned for several minutes—long enough for them to get on the interstate and head to Amarillo.

Brooke relished the absence of sound, the opportunity to gather her scattered wits back together. Take deep breaths, she instructed herself, hoping that tactic would settle her jittery nerves. And it actually helped, until Patrick opened his mouth again.

"Just so you know," he said. "There's no penalty for early payment on this debt of yours. By that I mean you can give me more than five kisses at a time, if you want to."

Good grief!

"Of course, the longer we drag this thing out, the more interest you'll owe."

Interest? "I'll think about it," Brooke promised, not verbalizing her belief that she'd probably dream about it, too.

"Did you get your help hired?" Patrick then asked, a question so normal that Brooke had trouble registering it.

"My...? Oh. Yes, I hired two young women, one three days a week, one four. I'll be there everyday, of course, at least at first."

"Don't overdo, Brooke," Patrick cautioned. "I've been there. I know it's an easy mistake to make."

"I'll be careful," she promised, even as he exited the van off the freeway again and headed down a road with which she wasn't familiar. "Where are we going?"

"My warehouse. I have televisions to let. You can borrow one until you can get what you want."

"That's very sweet," Brooke told him. "But entirely unnecessary."

"Hey," he responded. "I'm glad to help out."

Ten minutes later, Patrick drove into a huge parking lot on which sat trailers, boats, a tractor and a camper. He wasted no time in getting out of the van, and ever the gentleman, opened Brooke's door so he could assist her to the ground. Together they walked to the building, where Patrick unlocked the heavy metal door and ushered her inside.

On inspection, Brooke saw no one around anywhere. She did see things…lots of things, and her jaw
dropped at the sight of all that lay before her.

She saw furniture; she saw tools; she saw appli-
ances. She even saw a car—a very old car—that
looked like a vehicle her great-greats might have
courted in. She also saw an area equipped like an office.

"Where do you get all this stuff?" she exclaimed,
slowly pirouetting to take in the whole room.

"I buy some of it, loan money for some of it, trade
for the rest." Patrick walked to a corner of the building and pointed to a cluster of televisions in all shapes
and sizes. "Some of these I just keep for parts, but I
know this one and this one—" he indicated which sets
"—work perfectly. Which would go best with your
decor?" He grinned.

"Probably neither," Brooke replied. "But I'll take
that one." She pointed to a clean-looking portable.

With a nod, Patrick hoisted it up off the floor and
headed toward the front door, Brooke one step behind.

"See anything else you can use?" he asked when
he'd set it down on the floor again near the exit.

Once more, Brooke inspected her surroundings. "I
could use that lamp there, and that toaster. I'll pay you
for them, of course."

"Just add them to your bill," Patrick commented,
words that set her heart to racing.

"But I owe you too much already," she protested.

"Then maybe you'd better get started paying me back," he replied, stepping forward to wrap his arms around her in a hard hug.

Brooke, having wished for that hug all day, returned it full measure, just as she did the kiss he immediately gave her.

A marvelous kiss it was . . . tender, slow, ultimately erotic. Brooke forgot to breathe, forgot to think, forgot to fear. Instead she gave herself up to it, and as if sensing her surrender, Patrick groaned softly in response.

"There's a bed over there . . ." he whispered.

"I have one already," she replied, deliberately misunderstanding him.

"That's not what I meant." He tucked a finger under her chin, raising her gaze to his.

"I know, but I—"

"Never mind," he interjected. "I'm out of line."

Not as much as you think, Brooke silently replied, words she dared not utter aloud. Gently, she eased free of his embrace. "Maybe we'd better go."

He hesitated only a heartbeat before picking up the television and walking outside to the van. Alone in the warehouse, Brooke found herself loath to pick out anything else for her apartment, and not because she really thought Patrick might demand payment for it.

For the first time she had no desire to borrow someone else's mementos, someone else's memories.

For the first time she wanted to make some of her own.

"Where's the cable hookup?" Patrick asked Brooke a good three hours later, back in her apartment.

"Right here," she replied, pointing out the rubber-encased wires that would connect her borrowed television to the outside world.

He made short work of hooking up the set, then helped her position it to where she could see it from the couch.

"Thanks," Brooke murmured. An awkward silence followed, not the first in the past half hour, and to break it, she walked over to her refrigerator. "Would you like a glass of lemonade? I bought a jug a while ago."

"After we get this stuff put up," he said, then began to unload the groceries she'd just purchased.

Food shopping with Patrick had proved an interesting experience—from the moment he dropped a carton of eggs right to when the cashier asked Brooke if her "husband" intended to carry the sacks to the car.

Patrick had grinned, but not corrected the woman. And neither had Brooke. Why, she didn't know.

Since Brooke had purchased quite a bit—starting a new household required so much—it took several minutes to empty the sacks and clear her counter. She then poured the lemonade, which they carried outside to the deck.

The sun shone golden in a bright blue sky. Patrick sat on one of the wrought-iron chairs, but Brooke walked to the rail and breathed deeply of the afternoon air.

"Did you know that Amarillo air has been rated the cleanest in the nation for a city its size?" Patrick asked, as though reading her thoughts.

"That so?"

"Uh-huh." He took a sip of his lemonade, all the while watching her over the rim of the glass.

A bit disconcerted by his steady stare, Brooke gladly escaped to the door a moment later when Miss Dot called through it.

"Hello," she said to her landlady.

"Hello, hon," Dot replied, and handed her a letter. "Your mailbox is outside. Since I forgot to tell you about it, I just brought this on up."

"Thank you," Brooke said.

"I'd like to introduce you to the rest of my tenants. I was thinking we could all have cake and ice cream together later tonight, say, eight o'clock. You can bring your young man, of course." Dot peered over Brooke's shoulder at said young man, who waved at her.

"That's very nice, and if Patrick is still here I'll certainly bring him," Brooke replied.

Dot smiled at that, nodded and went on her way. Brooke, her attention on her letter, walked back out to the balcony. She sat next to Patrick and ripped open the envelope, which bore the logo of her insurance company. A check fell into her lap.

Brooke noted the amount and smiled at Patrick. "Thank goodness for insurance."

"Yeah," he agreed somewhat dryly.

Brooke read the letter accompanying the check. "Looks like the trailer rental company is going to get a new trailer, too. Unfortunately, the contents—all my personal things—aren't covered." She gave him a grim smile. "Well, at least I'll get some new wheels out of the deal. I'll start looking tomorrow. I already have a good idea what I want."

"Another convertible?" he asked.

"No," Brooke replied. "I never liked my other one."

"Why ever not?" Patrick asked, clearly astounded. "It was one sporty number."

"And a guilt gift from my dad."

Patrick frowned. "What do you mean, 'guilt gift'?"

"He gave it to me the night of my manager's school graduation ceremony. Drove it from Seattle to Portland, right to my front door, and handed me the keys." She laughed without humor. "I was so excited . . . but not because of the car. I couldn't believe he'd actually driven all that way to attend my banquet."

"I take it you and your father aren't close."

"That's the understatement of the year," Brooke told him.

Patrick narrowed his gaze. "Are you saying he . . . mistreated you?"

Brooke nodded. "My father never loved me," she said, going on to describe her childhood after the death of her mother—the nannies and housekeepers too numerous to recall, the private schools, the holidays spent with roommates.

She told Patrick about the fights with her stepmother, Judy, who was only eight years older than Brooke and fiercely territorial. She told him about her lonely college years and about her painful, but necessary, decision to move to Texas to start a new life, make a new home.

Dead silence followed her narrative, and Brooke smiled at Patrick, grateful for his sympathetic attention to her sad tale.

But he didn't smile back. "You're really very lucky, you know," he said instead, words that shocked her.

"Lucky? How can you say such a thing?"

"Did he yell at you? Hit you?"

"Of course not."

"Did he steal your money and spend it on booze and drugs? Did he chase away your friends? Insult your teachers? Abuse your mother?"

"No."

"Then you're lucky, Brooke Brady," Patrick said again. "Damned lucky."

"But he loves his stepson more than he loves me," she exclaimed, leaping to her feet and glaring down at him.

Patrick stood, too. "That's an assumption."

"Assumption, hell. It's the truth. Why else would he ignore me all those years?" Whirling, she walked back over to the balcony rail and sat on it, her back to the beauty of Amarillo.

"All those years, yes," Patrick agreed, joining her. "But what about this year? Maybe his showing up at your banquet means he has regrets. Maybe his talking about all those things he does with his son was just a way of telling you that he now knows what a father is supposed to do."

"*Step*son," Brooke corrected, refusing to consider for one moment this new idea. It wasn't one she wanted to hear. Patrick sighed in response, a sound Brooke found as annoying as the rest of their conversation thus far.

"You know what I think?" he asked.

"No," Brooke snapped, crossing her arms over her chest, studiously avoiding his probing gaze.

Patrick framed her face in his palms and forced her to face him again. "I think that you've nursed your grudge against your father for so long that you've become attached to it."

Brooke caught her breath, but said nothing.

"Hating him is much easier than loving him, isn't it, Brooke?" he taunted. "Just as making a new home here is easier than fighting for the one that's rightfully yours."

"No," she said, yanking his hands from her face. "That's not true."

"It is true. You're a coward, Brooke, and I'm here to tell you that you'll never be happy until you face life's challenges instead of running from them."

With a cry of pure outrage, Brooke pushed Patrick away and got to her feet.

"Thank you so much for your opinion, Mr. Expert On Fathers And Life," she said, then stomped to her door, which she opened. "Now if you'll please leave...."

Patrick, still standing on her balcony, winced, but did as requested, brushing by and exiting without so much as a backward glance.

Brooke immediately slammed the door hard, hoping with all her heart that it bruised his heels.

Brooke barely managed civility at Dot's little get-together that night, thanks to Patrick's no-nonsense lecture. She smiled politely to her neighbors, a married couple with no children, and another single woman, and chitchatted as though she really cared about their families, jobs, and problems.

Her mood had improved by so little the next day that car shopping, which should have been fun, proved to be a drag. But Brooke did order a vehicle that suited her—a rather sporty model in the most gorgeous shade of blue she'd ever seen—and was promised she'd have it by the next weekend since exactly what she wanted was on a lot in Dallas.

On Monday, shoe stock began to arrive at Ruby's Slipper. Brooke worked hard all day, sparing not one glance to the business next door. Unfortunately her thoughts weren't as easy to control and she found them on Patrick quite often.

For all her distraction, she accomplished much on Monday and on Tuesday in the way of inventorying shoes and training both her new workers in the rudiments of displaying merchandise, ringing up sales, and handling layaways and returns.

On Wednesday, she attended a mall managers' meeting to finalize plans for Saturday's grand opening. Patrick was present, of course, and by the luck of the draw, Brooke found herself seated directly across from him.

He looked fantastic in that jade shirt and those jeans, darn his hide. It was all she could do not to stare....and drool.

As the meeting progressed, she became aware of how much respect he commanded from the other managers. That made sense, of course. He had been around since the onset of this project. Nonetheless, she found the constant deferring to his opinion, the requests for his ideas, rather annoying. She had an opinion, too, and some darn good ideas.

"So what do you think, Patrick?" the rather portly manager of the Middle C music store asked, a question in keeping with Brooke's musings.

"I think free refreshments and balloons are probably enough," Patrick said. "We don't really need any clowns."

"But clowns add such an air of festivity," Brooke argued for no particular reason other than to hear an opposing point of view.

"And who's going to pay for these clowns?" Patrick asked her. "They don't come cheap, you know, and we've already overspent our grand opening budget."

"Maybe we could get volunteers," Brooke replied. "Maybe a senior citizens' group or something."

"Hey, great idea," someone murmured.

"Yeah," someone else added.

Brooke smiled sweetly at Patrick, whose steely gaze told her he didn't appreciate her opinion all that much.

"Are you going to coordinate it?" he asked.

Brooke's smile faded. "I'm not sure I can. I'm new to the area, you know."

"Anyone else want to do it?" Patrick asked in a tone so bossy it set Brooke's teeth on edge.

No one said a word.

He grinned rather cockily. "Then I guess we'll get along without clowns."

"Just a darn minute!" Brooke exclaimed, slapping her flattened palm on the massive conference table. "I didn't say I wouldn't do it."

"You didn't?"

"No, I didn't." She took a deep breath. "Even though I'm not familiar with the volunteer organizations around here, I'll coordinate clown roundup."

"It won't be easy," Patrick cautioned with not a little sarcasm.

"That's okay," Brooke assured him. "I love a good challenge."

That reply earned her a hoot of derisive laughter from her nemesis and, suddenly reminded of their conversation about cowards and challenges, she leaped to her feet in outrage.

"I'm telling you, I do!"

"Sure you do," Patrick responded dryly, getting up to glare at her across the table.

"Hold everything!" exclaimed the stately man seated to Brooke's left. He pointed to Patrick. "Sit down, sir."

Patrick did.

"And you," he then said to Brooke, who also obeyed. He reached for her hand and turned it palm side down, making a great show of examining her fingers.

"What are you doing?" demanded Patrick, his eyes narrowed, his body tensed.

"Looking for her wedding ring. I thought maybe you two were secretly married. God knows, you're acting like it."

Everyone laughed at that, a sound that naturally lightened the moods in the room.

"Sorry," Patrick murmured rather sheepishly when the noise died down. He loosened the neck of his shirt, the top button of which wasn't even secured.

"Me, too," Brooke added, every bit as embarrassed as Patrick appeared to be. Self-consciously, she smoothed her white linen pants and tugged at the sleeves of her navy jacket.

"That's okay," the peacemaker said, a kindly smile on his face. "We've all been working hard for months to get ready for this grand opening. It's only natural that tempers might be a little short. Shall we get back to business now...?"

Everyone agreed and the meeting progressed on a much lighter note. When it ended, the group quickly dispersed, leaving Patrick and Brooke alone.

"May I walk back with you?" he asked.

"Sure," she replied, leading the way back to their respective places of business.

Patrick said nothing more until they reached the door of Ruby's Slipper, at which point he gave her a half-smile.

"I think I owe you an apology."

"Actually, I owe you one," Brooke replied. "We probably don't need clowns."

"Oh, I'm not talking about that," Patrick said. "I mean about Saturday, about playing amateur psychiatrist." He shook his head. "I should never have opened my mouth. I, of all people, am in no position to offer advice on fathers."

That said, he spun on his heel and walked into The Electric Rainbow, leaving Brooke confused and curious as heck about his cryptic comment.

Chapter Eight

Brooke hesitated only a second before she followed him into his arcade for an explanation.

"What did you mean by that?" she asked, catching up and halting him by slipping her arm through his.

He turned to face her, his expression unreadable, and stood silent for long moments.

"Have I given you the grand tour?" he then asked, instead of answering her.

"Well, no...."

"Then by all means, allow me." Placing his hand over hers to keep it tucked at his elbow, he led her through a maze of video games, basketball challenges, skeetball lanes and various other electronic rides and gadgets. Brooke couldn't believe the variety of amusements offered.

"This is amazing," she murmured, impressed in spite of her prejudices. "Much bigger than any arcade I've ever seen."

"So you have visited one before?" He sounded surprised.

"Just once," Brooke admitted. "And only long enough for my fiancé to kiss me goodbye forever."

"He broke off your engagement in a video arcade?"

Brooke nodded. "He was that kind of guy. A real jerk."

"You once called me a jerk," Patrick reminded her.

"I didn't know you then," Brooke said, a candid reply that earned her one sexy grin. "Not that you don't still have a jerky day now and then."

"Hmm. Is this one of them?"

"Well, you weren't exactly on your best behavior at the meeting," she reminded him.

"As if you were."

She ignored that. "I'm not sure how to answer your question. I'll have to think on it."

"So think on it and tell me tonight at dinner, my place. Mother was not pleased that I didn't bring you in on Saturday when I dropped off the girls. I promised I'd ask you over tonight."

"That's very sweet," Brooke said. "But I can't. I have to work."

"Is it something I can help with?"

"It's book work," she replied. "And no one can do it but me . . . unfortunately."

"I know how that is," Patrick said.

"Will you thank your mother for me?"

"Sure." He released her hand and stepped back. "Guess I'd better let you go now. I have some book work of my own to do—book work I've been neglecting lately."

Taking that as her cue to leave, Brooke nodded and headed to the entrance. "Have fun," she teased as she stepped out of sight.

"Yeah, right," Patrick muttered to no one.

With a sigh, he, too, headed to the exit. He locked the door, then walked to his car. He hadn't exaggerated when he'd told Brooke he had book work to do. He did have. Tons of it that he'd neglected due to his preoccupation with his car wash, his video arcade, and . . . one sassy lady with honey-blond hair and sparkling hazel eyes.

At seven that night, Patrick still worked at his warehouse office. Around him lay a clutter of wadded papers, dull pencils with chewed off erasers, and empty soft drink cans.

How he hated balancing his bank statement—almost as much as paying federal income tax every quarter. He couldn't wait until his mother earned her accounting degree so he could turn all this over to her.

With a heartfelt snort of disgust, Patrick picked up his latest soft drink and took a swallow, nearly dropping the can when the phone rang and scared him out of his wits. He answered it with a growl of annoyance.

"Patrick? Sam Richardson here. I hate to bother you, but I'm trying to find the young woman whose red convertible landed on your car wash during that tornado weekend before last. You remember the woman—small, blond, easy on the eyes?"

"I remember," Patrick replied somewhat dryly to his old friend. "What's up?"

"We've found her trailer, the one she lost. Apparently the twister dumped it in Lawrence Bean's stock pond. He doesn't use that field anymore, so just now found it."

"What kind of shape is it in?"

"I think I can safely say that no one is going to be towing that baby anymore, but, oddly enough, there are still things in it. They'll be wet and muddy, of course, but maybe she'll be able to salvage some of it."

"That's great!" Patrick exclaimed, leaping to his feet. "Have you told her?"

"That's what I'm calling you about," the trooper said, going on to explain that he didn't have her address or phone number and hoped Patrick did since he'd heard she'd stayed at his place the night of the storm.

"Why don't I just tell her myself?" Patrick suggested.

"Fine with me," came the reply.

The second Patrick finished that call, he dialed Information and obtained the phone number for Ruby's Slipper, a brand new listing. But when he dialed it, no one answered.

After ten rings, Patrick gave up, called Information back and got Brooke's personal number. Obviously she'd taken her book work home. Patrick couldn't blame her for that. She spent too many hours at the shoe store as it was, to his way of thinking.

But she wasn't there, either.

Naturally assuming she must be between places, Patrick turned his attention back to his ledger for just long enough to give her time to get home. Then he called again . . . with no better luck.

Instantly he worried that something might have happened.

Or had she lied?

It wouldn't be the first time he'd been deceived by a woman who didn't have the guts to be honest. Was Brooke another of those women?

Was she trying to avoid him?

Or was there another reason she might have lied? Like, maybe, his family.

Patrick loved his family—every single eccentric member of it. His mother, brother, sister, nieces, uncle, and even his brother-in-law were an anchor. They kept him goal-oriented, busy, laughing, and sane. He needed them.

Unfortunately not everyone else shared his devotion. Stephanie certainly hadn't, a state of affairs he'd told himself would change over time but one that had, instead, grown worse.

Patrick would never forgive himself for the pain he'd inflicted on his loved ones by being so blind to Stephanie's treatment of them. But she'd been so clever, never saying or doing anything hateful when he was around.

He wondered to this day why she'd worked so hard to deceive him. Though well off, he wasn't the richest man in the state. He certainly wasn't the best looking, either.

Perhaps, at thirty-three, she'd been desperate enough to latch onto any man she thought could give her the things she wanted....

And, because of her treachery, because he'd been burned, he now found himself doubting the motives of a woman he loved.

Loved? Patrick sat bolt upright in his creaky old chair. Where in the hell had *that* come from?

He didn't love Brooke. He wanted her, sure. But sexual desire had nothing to do with love, and he well knew it.

No, he didn't love her, and it was a damned good thing since she obviously couldn't be trusted.

Just like Stephanie, she'd lie when the truth would serve better.

And just like Stephanie, she didn't like his family.

Having convinced himself of all that, Patrick closed his ledger with a snap, downed the rest of his drink, and strode out of the warehouse.

Moments later found him speeding home, grim-faced and steering with a white-knuckled clench. By the time he turned down his street some ten minutes later, he'd washed those knuckles clean of Brooke Brady for good.

No more would he hang around Ruby's Slipper begging for kisses.

No more.

Women were a dime a dozen in Texas, and he had lots and lots of dimes....

"Well, hell." Patrick hit the brake as he uttered those words and glared at the shiny blue sports car parked in his drive. Standing beside it were Brooke and every member of his family except Randy, still off in Nashville.

Frowning, he turned into the drive and leaped out of his car. Emmy and Shelly immediately ran up to greet him.

"Brooke's got a new car," Shelly said.

"She gave us a ride in it," Emmy said.

So Brooke didn't hate his family, after all. The sudden tightness of Patrick's stomach, the lurch of his heart told him he'd really been hoping that she did.

Why? he wondered, even as the answer came to him.

If Brooke couldn't deal with his family, he'd have the perfect excuse not to deal with her. But she *could* ... so he had to.

Damn.

"Hi, there," the woman in question called, waving gaily to him. "Want to go for a spin?"

"Um, sure," Patrick murmured, walking slowly forward.

"Hop in," Brooke said.

Patrick hesitated and looked hopefully around. "Anyone else going?"

"We just got back," Sarah replied for all of them.

Gulping, Patrick nodded, then crawled into the car, which smelled delectably new.

"Where to?" Brooke asked.

"You're driving."

"But I don't know my way around."

"Well . . . there's a lake not far from here. . . ."

"Point me in the right direction."

He did, and in another fifteen minutes Brooke wheeled to a stop by an inky-black lake flecked with moonbeams.

"Nice car," Patrick commented for lack of anything better to say when she killed the engine and shifted so she almost faced him.

"A dream to drive."

"I tried to call you awhile ago—at Ruby's Slipper and at home."

"Yeah?"

"You weren't there."

She laughed at what had to be the most idiotic thing he'd ever said. "I got the call on my car around six o'clock. I just couldn't wait to pick it up and show it off."

He nodded.

"Did you need me for anything in particular?" Brooke then asked. She looked a bit puzzled by his behavior. Patrick didn't blame her.

"Sam Richardson, the state trooper who picked you up on the highway when the tornado struck, called me. Your trailer has been found."

"My trailer . . . ? The one with all my things in it?" Her eyes were big as cupcakes.

"Yes. He called me because he didn't know—"

Brooke's squeal of delight obliterated Patrick's explanation. She threw her arms around his neck in a stranglehold he didn't have time to return, then beat the ceiling of her car with both hands, yelling "Yes! Yes! Yes!"

Patrick hurried to caution her. "He isn't sure how much was lost, Brooke. He just knows there are some things still in it." Patrick then explained where the trailer had been found and where it was now.

"I'll check it out first thing tomorrow," Brooke said, adding, "Will you show me where?"

"Sure."

Companionable silence reigned for about two seconds. Then Brooke opened her car door.

"Lets walk," she said as she got out.

Since that sounded like a fine idea to Patrick, he did the same. In another two seconds they strolled along the edge of the lake.

Overhead a brilliant moon and millions of stars, the only source of light, shone down on them. A slight breeze danced through the trees, from which tree frogs serenaded them and them alone. No one else was there.

Patrick, not oblivious to such a romantic setting, suddenly stopped walking and pulled Brooke into his arms.

"You still owe me seventy-five kisses," he murmured into her ear.

"Don't forget the ones I owe for my television, lamp and toaster," Brooke reminded him, much to his delight. "How much did those cost me?"

"Hmm." He made a big deal of calculating. "They're all secondhand."

"Yes."

"But all in excellent condition."

"Of course."

"Twenty-five more? That would make your debt to me an even hundred kisses."

"I can handle that," Brooke said. Patrick, who wasn't so sure *he* could, winced at her reply. "Shall we get started on them?"

"I'm game." Was he ever!

"One," she counted, brushing her lips over his. "Two." She did it again. "Three—"

"Hold it, hold it," Patrick interjected. "Those are not the kinds of kisses you owe me."

"Oh?"

"You don't remember our conversation in the stockroom."

She tipped her head back. "We talked in the stockroom?"

He grinned. "A word or two."

"Hmm. I seem to have forgotten them. Perhaps you'll explain again the kind of kisses you have in mind."

"Why don't I just demonstrate them?" Patrick replied, and then proceeded to do just that.

He put his heart and soul into the kiss. He erased past disagreements. He forgot past misunderstandings. He ignored future fears.

He tasted, teased and touched, cherishing her soft moans, her shivers and her sighs.

Finally he raised his head, ending the earth-shattering contact.

"Have I made myself clear?" he asked her, his voice husky with emotion.

She drew in a shaky breath. "Perfectly, and I now understand about your safety concerns, too, by the way."

"Do you like living dangerously, Brooke Brady?"

"I've never done it before," she replied, an answer Patrick believed.

"There's a first time for everything, I hear."

"Y-yes."

"So what are you going to do?"

She hesitated only a millisecond before wrapping her arms around his waist and laying her cheek on his thudding heart.

"Take a walk on the edge," she then whispered, words he heard loud and clear.

In one smooth motion, Patrick swept her up into his arms. He carried her to her car, where he deposited her on the hood, then pressed his body as close as possible. She parted her legs to accommodate him, wrapping them around his thighs, holding him just there while they kissed and touched.

With shaking hands, Patrick rid her of her jacket then raised her red silk shell up over her bra. He caressed her lace-covered breasts with his hands, giving loving attention to the tips, which hardened in response.

Unable to resist seeing that response, Patrick then unfastened the garment and eased the lace cups aside so he could feast his eyes on her skin, glowing soft and sexy in the light of the full moon.

At that moment Brooke began to push his shirt up over his chest. He let her, reveling in the brush of her fingers over his hypersensitive skin. She traced a heart over his with her fingertips, then kissed the pulse throbbing steadily in his neck.

That pulse went berserk in response. With a soft growl, Patrick pushed Brooke back on the car. She looked like a goddess lying there, he thought—hair spilling out over the shiny blue metal, breasts heaving with every ragged breath.

Desire hit him right below the gut—desire such as he'd never known. His gaze locked with hers, he unfastened her belt, then unbuttoned and unzipped her linen pants.

Not one word did she say, but Patrick heard her pant for air.

Bending down, he kissed her stomach, right above the waistband of her lacy bikini panties. She gasped and squirmed, then caught his face in her hands.

"Look at me," she murmured.

He did, lying on top of her so that their eyes were inches apart, his elbows taking his weight.

"I want you," Brooke then said. "Do you want me?"

"You can't tell?"

"Say it, Patrick."

"I want you," he whispered, wondering at her need to hear the words. Weren't his actions proof enough?

She said nothing for a moment, then sighed. "It's hard for me to believe."

"You can trust me."

"Can I?" she asked, studying his face. "Can I?"

"I swear it, Brooke."

At once she smiled, something very like love shining in her eyes. "You'd never hurt me, would you?"

Hurt her? No...not unless that *was* love he saw. If it was, then they had a problem. A big problem.

Brooke kissed him then, a long, slow kiss he felt clear to the heart of him—a heart that didn't love her. A heart that was too soft to let him take the chance that she might be confusing desire with love, might now expect more than he could ever give.

He tensed.

Brooke felt it and lowered her arms from around his neck.

"What's wrong?" she asked, studying him with a steady gaze.

"I—" For once, words escaped him.

"Never mind," she said, pushing him aside so she could sit. "I already know."

To Patrick's dismay, she slid off the car and turned her back to him while she refastened and straightened her clothes. When she reached for her jacket, he caught her arm and made her look at him.

"I'm not sure what you want from me, Brooke," he admitted.

"I want friendship from you," she replied. *"And nothing more."*

Those words echoed like a death knell in Patrick's head. And when Brooke skirted the front of her car, headed to the door, he stopped her again.

"Brooke, I—"

"It's okay, Patrick. Really." She smiled, then, a smile that didn't reach her eyes, and got into the car.

After a second's hesitation, Patrick did, too.

They rode home in silence. She stopped the car. He hesitated only fractionally, then got out.

"About tomorrow," he said.

"I'll call the state troopers and handle it myself," she replied.

And when they parted seconds later, her goodbye sounded chillingly final.

"What's wrong with me?" Brooke asked her reflection in the mirror not an hour later. She sat at an old-time vanity, the kind with a wide stool. This one had a rose-colored satin cover stained with the shades of countless tubes of lipstick, eyeliners, blushes—other women's memories, made while they prettied themselves for this or that dance or dinner date.

Would she ever have such memories?

In her present mood of self-pity, Brooke doubted it... at least not until she figured out why no man wanted her.

She looked passably pretty, she decided on close inspection. Regular features, if nothing outstanding. Healthy hair. The freckles might be a detriment, but those she could hide with makeup.

"So what's wrong with me?" Brooke asked again. There had to be something. Why, even her own father had rejected her, along with too many other men, the latest... Patrick.

At the thought of him, Brooke's heart twisted. She gnawed her bottom lip, a nervous habit long ago overcome, then abandoned her sad reflection to walk over to her bed and crawl into it.

Why this agony? she asked herself. Why this pain? She'd known Patrick only a matter of days and been careful in her dealings with him.

Careful? You call letting that man undress you "careful"?

With a groan of embarrassment, Brooke covered her face with her feather pillow as if that would shut out the voice of her loudmouthed conscience.

So she hadn't been as careful as she might've been. So what? No harm had been done. And since her attraction to Patrick was only sexual and therefore controllable, no harm would be done.

Especially not now that she'd verified once and for all what she'd always suspected: no man could love Brooke Brady.

And tomorrow, secure in this knowledge, she would get on with her life as planned weeks ago. She'd work hard, make a career for herself, and quit relying on the acceptance of others—especially mere mortal men—for her happiness.

Those words, easy to say, were almost as easy to believe, and Thursday morning actually found Brooke in better spirits. Not that she didn't experience a moment or two of depression. She did, but she shook each one off right up until the moment she drove up to the state trooper holding lot and saw her poor trailer, when her spirits soared for the first time in days.

Even more battered, covered with mud and who knew what else, it was barely recognizable, but she knew it on sight. Oh, yes. She knew it on sight and could have hugged the man on duty.

With his help, the badly twisted trailer was pried open enough to give her access to the contents. Brooke rummaged through everything and set aside her clothes, all washable; her dishes and cookware, thankfully unbreakable; and her books, warped but still readable.

Unfortunately most of the things that mattered most—photos, her diplomas, a scrapbook—were missing or damaged beyond recognition, and depression anew settled over Brooke like a mantle.

Being presented with a bill for rescue of the trailer didn't help it one bit, even though she planned to turn it over to her insurance agent.

Nonetheless, Brooke got herself together enough to work hard all that day and into the night checking in the shoes that continued to arrive and stocking shelves. Friday was no different and maybe even harder on Brooke, whose thoughts ricocheted from the tasks at hand, to Patrick, to her personal belongings, still lying in a pile on her kitchen floor because she didn't have time to do anything with them.

Though not a last-minute person by nature, Brooke handled her situation with skill, knowing that it was the irresponsible actions of another manager that necessitated this wild scramble to get ready for the next day's grand opening.

All over the mall, managers experienced similar headaches, but a late evening walk through the place on the eve of grand opening day revealed that the vast majority were ready and eager for the public to descend upon them.

As Brooke made her way to her car that night, she glanced across the huge lot, looking for Patrick's truck. Since he usually parked in the same area, she found it easily enough and felt not a little stab of regret.

He'd probably been at the arcade all day, she realized. And not once had he stuck his head in her door to say hello or ask about her things. That deliberate avoidance just reinforced his rejection and dissolved any last lingering doubts that Brooke might have misinterpreted his reluctance at the lake Wednesday night.

Though she knew it was for the best, Brooke actually cried in her chicken noodle soup when she finally sat down to dinner. That pitiful display prompted yet another lecture from her conscience, which sternly reminded her she was better off alone and free, with no man to answer to, no man to wait on and pick up after.

No man to touch and kiss. No man with whom to build a home and make babies.

Chapter Nine

Saturday morning found Brooke in a much better mood, whether from an amazingly good night's sleep or because the grand opening had finally arrived, she didn't know.

Grateful for the respite from her blue funk, she arrived at Ruby's Slipper an hour early to make one final inspection. Everything looked perfect, just as she'd thought, so when her help arrived they were able to spend the last ten minutes staring out the front door at the gaily dressed clowns walking about—volunteer clowns she'd recruited Wednesday evening from several local organizations.

For that reason, Brooke saw Patrick when he walked by en route to The Electric Rainbow. Her heart leaped right up into her throat, then fluttered like crazy, a reaction that threatened to steal her new-found peace.

Fortunately she didn't have time to moon over him long since her very first customer walked into the shoe store only seconds later. Brooke let her clerk handle the customer, choosing instead to stay behind the counter and critique performance.

It proved flawless and Brooke relaxed again and, for the first time, relished her achievement. The arrival of another customer soon put an end to that self-indulgence, but Brooke didn't mind. In fact, she welcomed each and every man, woman and child who passed through that morning, of which there was a gratifying number.

Some simply looked; some tried on; some bought; and some did all three. Brooke thrilled with every sale, admittedly hovering around the cash register just so she could hear the whir of it.

That was all she heard in the way of electrical noises, however, a fact she realized around noon. Patrick had spoken honestly when he said the activity in his arcade wouldn't be annoying.

And what activity. Brooke marveled at the number of children, teenagers and even adults who gravitated to The Electric Rainbow.

She found herself glad for Patrick, who was, after all, a very nice man. So what if he didn't want her? Neither did her own father.

On that thought—that very thought—Brooke looked up and found herself face-to-face with said father. She blinked, not quite able to believe her eyes.

"Hello, Brooke," he said in a voice undeniably familiar.

She gaped at him, taking note of those dear gray eyes, that silver-streaked hair, those broad shoulders. "Dad?"

"Have I changed so much in a month?" he asked.

Brooke, now clutching the counter for support, could barely reply. "N-no. Of course not. It's just that I—What in the world are you doing here?"

Jonathan Brady laughed then. "I've come to your grand opening, of course."

Since there was no *of course* to it, Brooke now couldn't believe her ears. "You were already in town for a meeting or something?"

"No. I flew in this morning just for this. I thought I'd take you to lunch—assuming managers get to eat— and then fly back tonight."

"You came two thousand miles just to take me to lunch?" Brooke blurted, a thoughtless response that erased her parent's smile.

"Can we go? I'd really like to talk to you."

"I—" She swallowed hard. "Of course we can. Let me get my purse." Belatedly, Brooke turned toward her clerk, who watched with much curiosity. "Anna Peck, this is my father, Jonathan Brady. I'd like to have lunch with him if you think you'll be all right alone."

"Hey, no sweat," the young woman replied, waving Brooke toward the door.

"Where's the best food around here?" Jonathan asked, extending his arm so that Brooke could slip her hand through it.

"I don't know," Brooke replied, still breathless with surprise. "They all just opened today." She considered for a moment. "Do you like Chinese food?"

"Love it."

"Then why don't we try the Dragon's Lair?"

"Sounds good to me."

Arm in arm they walked to the restaurant, situated a good distance from Ruby's Slipper. So thrilled was Brooke to be with her father that she didn't even think about Patrick when they strolled past The Electric Rainbow.

The Dragon's Lair, a beautifully decorated establishment, had few empty tables. Brooke whispered congratulations to the couple who owned it, then requested a table for two.

Neither she nor her father spoke again until seated, menus before them. Then both spoke at once.

"So how have you—?"

"So what have you—?"

Both laughed rather awkwardly.

"You first," Brooke prompted with a smile. "After all, you did fly two thousand miles just to talk to me."

"You sound so amazed," Jonathan replied.

"I am," Brooke admitted. "I thought you had Little League or Boy Scouts or something every Saturday."

"And no time for you?"

Brooke shrugged, but said nothing since the waiter had come to take their orders. They both decided on the special—guaranteed to be served in ten minutes or less.

"And no time for you?" Jonathan Brady repeated the moment they were alone.

"You've never had any before," Brooke rightly pointed out, meeting his gaze square on.

"May I tell you a story?" he asked, crossing his arms on the table before leaning slightly forward.

"I'm a little old for fairy tales, don't you think?"

"This isn't a fairy tale, Brooke. This is nonfiction... about a man whose wife was his world, a man who was so bitter and resentful when she was taken from him that he could think of no one's loss but his own." He paused.

"Go on."

"You know that man was me, and you know the result of my selfishness. What you don't know is how very sorry I am for all the years of self-indulgence and depression that kept me from sharing your life."

"Is that why you came to my banquet that night in Portland? To try to tell me all this?"

"Yes," her father said, clearly relieved that she had guessed the reason. She hadn't, of course, but Patrick had. And it was his theory she now shared.

"And the reason you talked about Frank so much was because you were trying to show me how much you'd changed."

"Exactly. You knew?"

"Not then." Again she waited for the waiter, who deposited steaming plates of sweet and sour chicken before them. "You really hurt my feelings that night," Brooke commented with candor when the waiter left.

"Is that why you took this job here in Texas?"

Brooke nodded.

"I'd intended to ask you to live with me in Seattle, you know. That's one of the reasons I came to your banquet. I was going to remodel the garage apartment."

"You were?" Her eyes brimmed with tears.

"Yes. I thought we could start over, be friends." He laughed without humor. "I guess that was a lot to ask of you. Anyway, I'm sorry if I hurt you. I never meant to. I'll never knowingly do it again."

Brooke, nearly overcome, barely managed a nod and blinked rapidly to clear her vision. She found her father looking at her, an unreadable expression on his face.

"What is it?" she asked, sensing a certain disquiet.

"I can't get over how much you look like your mother," he replied, words that thrilled her more than she'd ever have imagined or he could ever know. "Same hair, same eyes, same freckles." He smiled. "Same temper, too, I'll bet."

"I don't have a temper."

"This from the child who once hid a quarterly report because I worked on it instead of taking her to the zoo?"

"I did that?"

"You know good and darn well you did, and I'll bet you remember where you put it, too."

Brooke, her mouth full of chicken, didn't reply for a moment, then admitted, "The clothes hamper." She shrugged. "I was jealous of Judy and the baby. You always had time for them, you know."

"You don't like Judy, do you?"

"No," Brooke admitted.

"I think you'll change your mind about her when you get to know her better. And speaking of that . . . I talked to your boss for a long time last week when I called to get the information about this grand opening."

"Yeah?"

"Yeah," Jonathan mimicked. "He assured me that if you would rather be in Seattle, he could arrange for a transfer. That position hasn't been filled yet, you know."

"I didn't know."

"So what do you say, Brooke? Come home with me? Give me a chance to make up for lost time? I swear you won't regret it."

"But I just signed a two-year lease on my apartment."

"I'll buy it out."

"But what about my friends . . . ?"

"You've only been here two weeks. How many friends could you have?"

"Several," she assured him with a sassy nod.

Her irritation was not lost on her father, who had the grace to wince. "Of course, you have friends. But you have more of them out west."

Brooke sighed. "True."

"At least think about it," Jonathan said. "You don't have to make a decision now. You'll always have a home with us."

"'Us' meaning you, Judy and Frank?"

"That's right."

Brooke sighed again. "I'd be less than honest if I told you I want to be around either of them. I have a lot of hard feelings against both and—" she looked him dead in the eye "—against you. It's going to take more than one lunch for us to erase twenty years of non-communication."

Jonathan considered that. "But we've made a start."

"We've made a good start," she agreed. "And even if I don't move back to Seattle, even if I don't ever like Judy or Frank, we'll still be a family, you and I."

"We will," he assured her, adding, "I love you, baby." Words that warmed Brooke's heart, did wonders for her self-esteem, and kept her on cloud nine throughout the rest of their meal.

Oblivious to the noise all around him, Patrick Sawyer paced the length and breadth of his arcade, automatically exchanging quarters for the tokens that activated all the games in his establishment.

He glanced at his watch and noted the time—one-thirty—then walked to the front of The Electric Rain-

bow from where he peeked into the shoe store next
door.

As with every other time he'd done the same thing,
he saw a roomful of customers and one clerk. No
manager, just one clerk.

Unable to bear the suspense any longer, Patrick
charged into the store and right over to the counter,
where he stopped beside the busy salesclerk.

"May I speak to you for a moment?"

"Just as soon as I finish up with this customer, sir,"
she replied without so much as a glance his way.

Though tempted to yank her back into the stockroom so he could get some answers, Patrick controlled himself for the five minutes it took her to
meticulously ring up her sale, package the merchandise and hand it to her customer with a smile and a
polite "Come again."

At that point she turned to him. "Now then, sir,
what can I do for you?"

"I want to know about the man Brooke left with
around noon," Patrick replied. "Who was he?"

The clerk, whose name was Anna according to her
name tag, eyed him somewhat suspiciously for a moment. "I'm not sure I should give out that information. Maybe if you told me who you are ... ?"

"A ... friend," Patrick replied. "I own the video
arcade next door."

Apparently that answer wasn't good enough. At any
rate, Anna didn't get in any big hurry to tell him about
Brooke's mysterious companion.

"I'm sure she'll be back in a few minutes." She gave him a polite smile. "Why don't you just ask her yourself?"

"Because I can't wait that long!" Patrick blurted, flushing when he added, "I'm worried about her. I've never seen that man around here before."

Anna studied his face then, studied it and smiled again, this time with sympathy. "There's no need to worry. The man was her father. He took her to lunch."

Her father? Relief washed over Patrick that the man in question—early fifties and damned handsome—was Brooke's father and not the fiancé who'd jilted her in the arcade now come back to rekindle an old romance.

Her father. Good. Very good. Maybe the two of them would mend a few broken fences over lunch. He sincerely hoped so. Though he didn't love Brooke, he still cared enough about her to want her to be happy.

With murmured thanks to Anna, who turned immediately to her next customer, Patrick stepped outside just in time to see Brooke and her father coming back from lunch. He slipped quickly into his arcade and, through the window, watched their approach.

Brooke looked more beautiful than he'd ever seen her—animated, smiling, eyes shining with happiness.

At once, regret nearly knocked him to his knees. That emotion, so powerful, caught him by surprise, just as his intense jealousy had earlier when he'd first seen Brooke and that strange man stroll by the arcade.

Jealousy? Regret? Weren't those emotions reserved for lovers?

Of course they were, and Patrick immediately reassessed his feelings for Brooke.

He found desire right off the bat—mind-boggling desire that kept him awake at nights and made cold showers a part of his daily routine. He also found honest affection—the friendship kind, the caring kind.

Was that all? he wondered, delving into the deepest corners of his heart to the no-man's-land unexplored since Stephanie's brief visit there years ago. There, hidden far from his view, lay love, too afraid to make itself known to him.

"Damn," Patrick muttered, suddenly so weak he had to lean against the glass. He hadn't expected to find love.

But there it was, and now discovered, it wouldn't be easily relegated to anonymity again.

No, indeed. In fact, Patrick already felt a change in himself, a lift of spirits, a burning need to go somewhere—like maybe next door—and do something—like talk to Brooke.

Just what he would talk to her about, he didn't know since he could hardly blurt the cold hard facts. An *I love you* from him, especially after their little fiasco on Wednesday night, might be difficult for her to accept.

So we'll take this slow, he told himself. *I'll walk over there, ask about her dad, chitchat, and then tell her what a fool I've been. We'll mosey back to the stockroom, shut and bolt the door, kiss...*

But here reality reasserted itself. There would be no hanky-panky in the stockroom today. Brooke was far too busy and a stockroom fling—assuming she'd ever agree to one—wasn't what he wanted anymore anyway.

He wanted a wedding. He wanted "I do," cake, friends and family. He wanted a honeymoon—boy did he ever want that!—and he wanted forever.

Brooke's forever.

He'd turn his house over to his mother and build Brooke one of her own. Families were nice, after all, but privacy was nicer.

They'd make a home, the two of them. They'd have children....

"Excuse me, sir?"

Patrick started, then looked down rather blankly at the youngster tugging on his shirt.

"I need some tokens," the boy said, holding out a handful of quarters.

With a brisk nod, Patrick abandoned his fantasies.

And fantasies they were, he realized seconds later when one of his video games broke down and reality of life and living hit hard. Brooke, who from all appearances had made up with her father, had not made up with Patrick Sawyer.

If he walked next door to try to tell her about his change of heart, she probably wouldn't listen. In fact, she might throw him out on his ear.

And that was okay, now that he thought about it. Secure as he now was in his love, a little thing like a bruised ear amounted to nothing and certainly wouldn't dampen his spirits or lessen his resolve to woo and win Brooke Brady.

The clock on the wall of The Electric Rainbow said four-thirty before Patrick found another free minute. Handing his fanny pack of tokens to his assistant, a trained transfer from one of his other arcades, Patrick walked right over to Ruby's Slipper and found Brooke alone...if you didn't count the two pre-teen girls trying on high heels.

Since those young girls didn't look anxious to actually make a purchase, Patrick walked right up to the counter, where Brooke stood writing.

"Hi, there," he said, his hungry eyes taking in every detail from her hair—loose today—to her shoes—attractively styled, but sensible enough to wear all day.

She looked up when he spoke and gave him a big smile.

Up until that moment, Patrick hadn't realized how much he'd missed that smile the past few days. Now he warmed in the glow of it.

"Hi, yourself," she said. "How's opening day at The Electric Rainbow?"

"Can't complain," he said. "How's yours?"

"A red letter day...for lots of reasons."

Though Patrick well knew those reasons, he wanted to hear them from her. He looked around. "Where's your help?"

"On break. She'll be back in—" Brooke glanced at her watch "—two minutes."

"You're so sure?"

"Uh-huh," she answered with a light laugh. "My break is next and I threatened her with her life if she took it, too."

"Do you have plans for your break?" Patrick asked, suddenly inspired.

"Sitting down," Brooke admitted, with a glance at shoes that might not be as comfortable as Patrick had imagined.

"Any place particular in mind?"

"No." She hesitated for just a heartbeat. "Are you on break, too?"

Patrick nodded and held his breath, hoping, waiting....

"Want to come with me wherever I go?"

He exhaled and grinned. "Yes."

In exactly two minutes—as predicted—Anna burst back into the store, downright breathless. "Thought I was going to be late," she explained, slipping into place behind the counter.

"Have you met the owner of The Electric Rainbow?" Brooke asked her clerk, moving over to stand next to Patrick.

"Sort of," Anna replied, eyes twinkling, a reply that produced a frown from Brooke and prompted Patrick to as good as drag her to the exit.

"I'll be back in ten minutes," Brooke called as he hustled her out the door and to the nearest chairs, which proved to be an ice cream parlor three doors down. She bought a cone, as did Patrick, then sat down with a heavy sigh. "What a relief. My first break since lunch."

"What did you do for lunch?" Patrick asked, grabbing the opening she handed him on a silver platter. "I tried the deli at the north end of the mall."

"I went to the Dragon's Lair," Brooke told him, eyes shining when she added, "with my dad."

"Your dad!" Patrick gave his performance all he had. "He was here?"

"In the flesh," Brooke replied, then went on to tell him about what sounded like a companionable dinner. "He was going to fly home tonight, but I talked him into staying over. My couch makes into a bed. I gave him the key to my apartment."

Lucky Dad, Patrick thought.

"He knows we won't be able to visit much tonight since I'll be working late, but I'm going to give him a tour of the city tomorrow morning before the store opens—what part of it I'm familiar with, anyway. I thought that would help him understand why I don't want to move back to Seattle."

Patrick nearly choked on his bite of pecan praline ice cream. "What do you mean move back to Seattle?"

Brooke shrugged. "He wants me to come home...be a part of his family."

"And you said no, of course."

"Not exactly, since the idea does have merits. But if I move back it won't be any time soon. I've commitments here. Among them—" she grinned "—a two-year lease."

Patrick digested that along with his frozen treat—or tried to. With his stomach in knots, it wasn't all that easy. "I take it you two have made up."

"As much as possible considering we've been strangers for a good twenty years. A relationship as rocky as ours won't be set to rights in a hour, you know. We'll both have to work at it. I'll have to try to get over my prejudices against Judy and Frank. He'll have to get used to the fact that I probably won't ever think of them as family."

So they still had their problems. Good, he thought in a fit of little boy insecurity. That meant Brooke wouldn't be in any hurry to pack up and move home.

Pack up?

"Did you have any trouble finding the holding lot?" Patrick blurted, suddenly reminded of Brooke's trailer.

"I made a couple of wrong turns, but I found it okay."

"I should've gone with you," Patrick murmured.

"I think that under the circumstances, it was best I go alone," she murmured, finishing up her cone.

"Circumstances as in what happened Wednesday night?"

"Mmm-hmm." She glanced at her watch and stood. "Break's over, or will be by the time we walk back." That said, she began walking back toward the shoe store.

Patrick leaped to his feet and hurried after.

"About that . . ."

"What?"

"Wednesday night. I think I owe you an apology."

"Don't be silly," she replied without sparing him so much as a sidelong glance. "We simply misread each other's signals, that's all. Happens all the time in man-woman games."

Games? She thought he was playing games?

Damn. Obviously this was going to be even harder than he thought.

Patrick grabbed Brooke's arm, halting her. "Brooke, I—"

At that instant the sound of shouting rang out. Startled, Patrick whirled around, scanning the area.

Almost immediately he spotted a commotion of some kind...right in front of The Electric Rainbow. He saw his assistant, waving madly to him; he saw a cluster of curious customers, watching with interest; and he saw a man, tall, belligerent, and looking for all the world as if he'd love to raise a little hell with someone.

Without another word, Patrick dropped Brooke's arm and headed that way to volunteer for the position.

Chapter Ten

Suddenly afraid for him, Brooke followed at a dead run. Heart thudding with fear, hands trembling, she watched as Patrick skillfully defused what could have been an explosive confrontation between his assistant and the man, who appeared to be three-sheets-to-the-wind drunk with tequila, judging from the bottle he waved around.

How he'd ever managed to get into the building with the liquor, Brooke couldn't imagine and vowed to bring up the subject at the next mall-wide managers' meeting.

Luckily, Patrick, ever cool and looking dashingly dangerous, parted the man from his bottle and, moments later, sent him on his way accompanied by his son, a teenager who'd just burst out of The Electric Rainbow, clearly mortified.

Brooke breathed a sigh of relief when the altercation ended without anyone getting hurt. She walked over to Patrick, hoping they could continue their conversation, but could see that he'd lost his train of thought.

And no wonder. He now had an arcade full of hyperactive teenagers and youngsters to corral. Since Brooke, who didn't envy him his task, didn't want to distract him, she just waved goodbye and headed next door to Ruby's Slipper.

Too bad, she thought, quite disappointed they weren't going to finish what had started out as an interesting dialogue. Clearly Patrick had had second thoughts about Wednesday. Why else would he bring up what was a painful memory for both of them?

What kind of second thoughts was the question, and Brooke desperately wanted the answer.

Lunch with her dad had done much for her self-esteem. His vow of love—so long in coming, so long desired—had performed a miracle. She found that she had new confidence in herself, much needed confidence. She had new courage, too, maybe even enough to fight for what she wanted most in the world.

A certain man.

Patrick.

For today's lunch had taught Brooke two lessons. First, she wasn't as unlovable as she'd always believed and, second, home was not in Seattle, Washington.

Just where home was, Brooke still didn't have a clue. Amarillo looked good at the moment but, like Seattle, was only a city. And her apartment, though nice, was only a roof over her head.

So where was home?

Brooke just wished she knew.

Brooke's watch said nine forty-five when she finally packed her bank bag, tucked it and her purse under her arm, and exited Ruby's Slipper.

Since Anna only worked nine to five, Brooke had handled the last four hours until closing time—9:00 p.m.—alone. Much busier than expected, those hours were, and every bone in her body now ached because of them.

Brooke inserted her key into the lock and secured the door with a flick of her wrist. With a weary sigh, she turned and found herself face-to-face with...a man. A tall man, who looked disconcertingly familiar.

"E-Excuse me," she stammered, startled half out of her wits. She moved to step aside, a move matched by the man, whose surly scowl she suddened recalled.

She gulped, not thrilled to find herself face to face with that afternoon's troublemaker.

"What time does that place close?" he demanded, pointing to The Electric Rainbow.

"Not for a couple of hours yet," Brooke told him, a bold-faced lie. In reality, the arcade closed at ten, but she hoped the man, who just might be hanging around to get even with Patrick, would be discouraged and move along.

"Damn," he muttered, swaying and staggering just enough for her to slip by.

Taking advantage of her opportunity, Brooke quickly sidestepped him, only to find herself grabbed by the upper arms and pulled up close.

"Looks like I've got myself an hour to kill, little lady. Why don't the two of us go somewhere real private and have a little fun?"

Thoroughly disgusted, but not yet scared—this was a very public place, after all—Brooke tried to break free. When she couldn't, she tipped her head back as far as she could to keep from smelling his breath—foul with the scent of whiskey.

"I really can't tonight," she replied, trying to keep the disgust out of her voice so as not to rile him further. "I've been on my feet all day and I'm just exhausted. Maybe another time?"

He laughed, then, a sound that made the hairs on the nape of her neck stand on end.

"Not another time," he growled, narrowing his gaze. "*Now*. I'll make you forget all about them pretty little feet of yours."

"No thanks," Brooke snapped, abandoning any further attempts at diplomacy. Once again she struggled to get free, a move that made him tighten his grip painfully.

Actually alarmed for the first time, Brooke caught her breath and looked all around, not quite believing that no one could see what was happening. She spied not a soul and was astounded...until she remembered the late hour.

Everything in Eastgate Mall but the movie theater and Patrick's arcade closed at nine. There might not be more than a handful of people in the entire mall and the theater was way at the other end of the building.

But the arcade wasn't.

Heart suddenly full of hope, Brooke glanced toward The Electric Rainbow. But the door was closed to keep down the noise level, just as Patrick had promised, and she could see nothing but video games through the windows—no patrons and no Patrick.

"I never take no for an answer," her assailant said, once more swaying and staggering. His off-balance step caught Brooke by surprise, and she stumbled with him.

With a move born of pure reflex, she clutched the man's arms so they wouldn't fall. Clearly misinterpreting her action, he laughed in unmistakable triumph, pulled her closer, and nuzzled her neck with his lips.

"Stop it!" Brooke exclaimed, at once thoroughly frightened. "Let me go!"

But he only laughed again and hustled her, struggling every step of the way, down the walkway. "I've got a bottle in my truck. Lets us go there."

Then and only then did the true danger of Brooke's situation really hit home. At once terrified out of her mind, she screamed as loud as she could—screamed and kicked her captor, hard, right in the shin.

He never even flinched.

And still no one came.

Brooke's head spun; her stomach churned. Her legs felt like dead weights.

Her surroundings turned gray and then black and, for the second time in her life, began to close in on her.

"You son of a bitch!"

Patrick's yell of fury yanked Brooke back from the brink of unconsciousness. She found herself free, and so unexpected was that release that she fell hard on the floor, where she lay stunned and panting while Patrick dealt with her assailant.

And deal with him he did. Brooke winced at the sound of flesh meeting flesh as they struggled. It was like a scene from a B Western or, more like it, her worst nightmare, since the man she loved was involved and, from the look of things, getting beaten to a pulp.

Brooke struggled to rise, movement hampered by her straight skirt. When she did get to her feet and surge forward to help, Patrick's "Out of the way, Brooke!" sent her scurrying...but not too far off.

They fought like wild men, Patrick and the drunk, and after only seconds both had bloody noses. Brooke, nearly beside herself with fear, began to scream again—this time with amazing results.

Around one corner dashed a security guard. Down the hall bounded two more.

Near tears, Brooke watched while they separated the fighters, both exhausted and neither a winner as far as she could tell since they both looked pretty darned awful.

As quickly as possible, Brooke told the officers what had happened.

They asked if she would press charges. She promised she would—someone had to get that man off the streets—but only later, after she made sure Patrick was all right. That satisfied the officers, who then escorted Brooke's attacker down the hall.

The minute they turned their backs, Brooke rushed right to Patrick and threw her arms around him in a bear hug. He staggered, then rallied enough to hug her back. But when she tried to kiss him, he dodged the caress.

"I'm bleeding."

And so he was, down his chin, all over his shirt.

"Oh, Patrick," she murmured, unaware of the tears streaming down her cheeks.

Patrick, however, took note of them right away.

"Did that bastard hurt you?" he demanded, tenderly brushing them away with his thumb. His anxious eyes studied her as though looking for bumps or bruises.

"I'm okay," she assured him.

Then she took his hand and led him back to Ruby's Slipper to the bathroom, where she lowered the lid on the toilet and made him sit while she tended to his face with water from the sink nearby.

"You're a mess," Brooke commented several seconds and wet paper towels later.

"I may look like hell," Patrick responded. "But I feel pretty damn good."

"You mean playing macho man agrees with you?"

"Macho man?" He gave her a pleased grin.

"You were an animal," Brooke told him as she gently bathed his upper lip in cold water. "I'd never have believed you could be capable of so much violence."

"Obviously you don't know me as well as you think."

"Obviously," Brooke said, silently adding, *but enough to love you like crazy.* "So tell me about yourself, Patrick Sawyer, starting with where you learned to swing like that. Were you a child of the streets who had to fight for his life every day?"

She said the words in jest, knowing what a secure youth he must have had, expecting him to laugh.

But he didn't laugh at all. "I was the child of a drunk and I never fought back...until I turned fourteen. Then my dear old dad hit my mother one time too many. When I got through with him that night, he was glad to leave us. And when I told him I'd kill him if he ever came back, he knew I meant it."

Patrick's voice, so cold, so emotionless, frightened Brooke almost as much as the dangerous glint in his eyes.

"I—I didn't know," she stammered, appalled that she had unwittingly resurrected such painful memories.

"Of course you didn't."

"And that jackass who attacked you awhile ago didn't know about the promise I made to myself the night I kicked my old man out of the house for good."

"What promise?" Brooke asked, laying aside her towel.

"I vowed that no one would ever again hurt someone I love."

Someone he loved?

Heart hammering, Brooke seated herself lightly on Patrick's knee. She hugged him, oh so grateful he wasn't hurt, then heaved a heartfelt sigh when he hugged her back and rested his chin on the top of her head.

"Am I someone you love?" she breathed into his neck, her newborn courage mysteriously vanished now that she needed it most.

Patrick tensed. She heard his convulsive swallow and smiled, at once aware she wasn't the only nervous one in the tiny room.

He leaned back slightly so he could see her better, tucking his fingers under her chin and turning her face to the light. With visible angst, he studied her expression and to aid him, Brooke put all her love there so he could see it.

"You are," he finally said. "Am I someone you love?"

"You are," she echoed without hesitation.

Patrick caught his breath, as though her answer surprised him. Then, with a whoop that even extra-thick walls couldn't contain, he leaped to his feet, taking her with him as he burst out of the bathroom to the store proper.

There, he spun her around, laughing like a crazy man...or maybe just one in love. And every bit as joyful, Brooke shared in that wonderful, warm laughter.

It wasn't until later—after many kisses, a trip to the police station and a trip to the bank's night depository—that Brooke heard the rest of his story.

Seated beside him on her couch, her very-interested Dad nearby, she coaxed the tale from Patrick with difficulty. Whether because of her father's presence or because Patrick didn't like to talk about his past, she didn't know.

His story wasn't a pretty one. Patrick had overcome incredible odds to keep his family together, to make them a home. Since his mother had no marketable skills to speak of and had never worked, he actually supported everyone from the tender age of fourteen. Brooke found that feat astounding and learned new appreciation for Patrick as well as for her father, who wasn't all that bad in comparison to Patrick's renegade parent.

It was some time after Patrick's confession, standing alone out on her balcony, that Brooke really had a chance to think about all he'd told her. Peeking in on the two men in her life, talking business like the financial wizards they both were, she analyzed her current state of mind and heart.

She felt warm.

She felt secure.

She felt loved.

Feelings that were all anyone could ask, Brooke realized. Feelings that told her she'd finally found the home she'd been seeking for ever and a day.

And where was home? Why, not a place at all, but a who—a precious, precious who, skilled in the art of survival, living and loving.

Home was a man who could teach her so much.

Home was Patrick Sawyer.

Epilogue

"Look at my hair," Brooke exclaimed, frowning at her reflection in the mirror of Sarah Sawyer's vanity. "It looks just awful."

"Your hair is beautiful," Cynthia replied from where she stood to Brooke's left.

"But my gown," Brooke then said. "It doesn't fit right through here." She traced her midriff with her hands. "I should have had it seamed in."

"Your dress is beautiful, too," Sarah replied from behind her. "And it fits perfectly."

"Should I take off the pearls? I mean, are they right with this style gown?" Brooke then questioned.

"They're perfect," Ruby Lloyd, who'd flown in the day before, assured her.

"Are you scared to get married?" ask Emmy, leaning on Brooke's knee, eyes wide with awe. Since she and her sister were both dressed in mauve today, Brooke had to rely on the tiny loop of blue satin ribbon on her lace collar for a positive ID.

"Yes," Brooke readily admitted."You don't want to be Uncle Patrick's wife?" Shelly asked from her position at Brooke's other knee.

"Of course I do—more than anything," Brooke told her. "I just wish we'd eloped or something."

"That would've been easier," Sarah murmured as she placed a beaded cap atop Brooke's head and then arranged the veil flowing from it.

Easier? By far. And since Brooke Brady no longer took the easy way out, she now faced a wedding complete with all the trimmings . . . not the least of which was a roomful of guests.

Brooke gulped, stood, and faced her faithful friends. "How do I look?"

"You're the most beautiful bride I've ever seen," Sarah told her with utter sincerity, and then burst into tears. Cynthia immediately did the same.

"Don't do this to me," Brooke wailed, even as Ruby, who laughed instead of cried, ushered everyone out of the room except the flower girls, who watched the proceedings in utter fascination.

"Are you girls ready?" Ruby asked Emmy and Shelly.

They picked up their bouquets and nodded solemnly.

"Brooke?"

Brooke, busy repairing her mascara, tossed the smeared tissue into the trash and nodded, too, rather tremulously.

"Then I'll go downstairs and signal the preacher."

She did, and immediately Brooke heard the muted refrains of the country love song she and Patrick had selected for their ceremony.

Outside low thunder rumbled and heavy rain pelted the windows, but caught up in the moment, Brooke felt no fear at all.

She moved to the top of Patrick's stairs, the banisters of which were beautifully decorated with a garland of flowers, then carefully descended them, ever conscious of her floor-length skirt and the trail of lace and pearls behind her.

At the door of Patrick's living room, Ruby stood awaiting her musical cue. Brooke smiled at her long-time friend, who winked, then entered the room, walking slowly down an aisle lined with chairs, friends and family.

Calm settled over Brooke, welcome, much-needed calm. She took the arm her father extended to her, moved to the doorway, and immediately spotted Patrick, standing between his preacher and his brother, the long-lost Randy, at the altar.

He smiled at her and his eyes shone with love.

Brooke smiled back and, her own eyes ever on him, began to walk the aisle with her dad....

"Attention all units! Attention all units! We have a tornado. Man your posts!"

Brooke stopped short even as Patrick started, said something to the preacher and vanished through the dining-room door. All around her, their guests, many of them from Oregon and Washington, whispered and stared. The pianist, clearly uncertain about what to do, just sat there, hands frozen over the keys.

Brooke moved not a muscle, either, but waited patiently, well aware of Patrick's responsibility when he received a call on the emergency radio that was never turned off.

She was rewarded for her patience seconds later when Patrick burst back through the door.

"Sorry, folks, but we're going to have to put this wedding on hold for a bit," he said. "Seems we've got ourselves a Texas twister to deal with right now. I'd like all of you to head to the basement, if you will. Just open that door right over there—that's the one, sir— and be careful of the stairs going down."

While their guests, visibly frightened, scurried to the basement, Patrick made his way over to Brooke.

"Stay with me," he ordered, laying an arm over her shoulders, taking her from her father.

"You don't have to leave?"

"I'm excused from duty today, and there isn't time, anyway. It's almost on us, honey."

Brooke caught her breath and nodded, letting him guide her to the stairs. In moments, everyone stood clustered below, illuminated by the light of a single bulb swaying at the end of a wire suspended from the ceiling.

They all talked at once and someone sobbed. Brooke, fully sympathetic with their fears—especially those of her northwestern friends—turned to Patrick.

"Do something," she whispered.

He nodded and, taking her hand, lead her through their guests to the far end of the massive concrete room. There he whistled sharply to get everyone's attention over the racket.

"Excuse me," he said, his voice ringing loud and clear. "May I have your attention, please?"

Finally silence settled over the group. That silence increased the intensity of the storm raging outside, of course, but Brooke still felt no fear. If her life ended today, she would have no regrets.

Patrick had already made her happier than she'd ever believed possible.

"Since we have a few extra minutes, here," Patrick continued, "I thought I'd tell you all a story."

"Oh, goody." Brooke recognized Emmy's voice. "I love stories."

Her comment produced laughter all around and lowered the panic level just a bit. Brooke noted, with vast relief, the presence of some smiles.

"And this story is a dandy," Patrick said. "Full of adventure. Full of romance." He grinned mischievously at Brooke. "Shall I begin?"

"Please," answered a female guest, obviously intrigued. Apparently she wasn't the only one. Brooke now noted that every gaze in the room rested on Patrick.

"Once upon a time there was a young woman who ran away from home," he began, words that caused Brooke to exchange a sheepish glance with her grinning father. "Along the way, she met up with a tornado."

"Are you telling the *Wizard of Oz?*" Shelly suddenly interjected.

"He's talking about Brooke," Emmy informed her with a huff of superiority, a reply that produced even more laughter.

Patrick never batted an eye. "Our young woman and that mean ol' twister collided head-on, and not surprisingly the twister won. The prize was...her pretty red car."

Since everyone present had long since heard of Brooke's little adventure, they all looked at her and laughed. But it was the laughter of love, and so she laughed with them.

"That old twister must not have liked that car much, because it spit it out shortly after...right on some poor old joker's car wash."

"That's you!" Emmy exclaimed.

"Yeah." He grinned. "The young lady and joker didn't get along very well at first. In fact, she didn't like him much at all, and he didn't like her, either—at least that's what he told himself. In reality, he probably fell in love the very first moment he laid eyes on her."

"Oh, Patrick," Brooke murmured, taking the tissue a thoughtful someone thrust upon her. With it she dabbed at her damp mascara again.

Patrick smiled at her, wiped his own eyes and sighed rather lustily. "Anyway, to make a long story short, they finally realized how they felt about each other and—"

"Here they are!" Emmy and Shelly both proclaimed.

"Yeah," he said, his voice husky with emotion. "Here they are, waiting on another tornado to get gone so they can get married."

"Why wait?" a guest suddenly asked.

"Yeah," another piped up. "Why wait? You've got the preacher. You've got us. Are you going to let a little ol' twister get the best of you?"

Patrick looked at Brooke, who laughed up at him.

"Well . . . are you?" someone else demanded.

"Not me," Patrick replied.

"Or me," Brooke added.

In seconds, she found herself at the other end of the room from where Patrick once more waited with the preacher.

Their guests divided into two groups and parted, leaving an aisle down which the flower girls and Ruby Lloyd slowly walked.

Then, with the rain pattering a wedding march on a tiny solitary window, Brooke and her dad walked that same aisle, all smiles, and headed straight for her happily ever after.

*   *   *   *   *

OFFICIAL RULES • MILLION DOLLAR BIG WIN SWEEPSTAKES
NO PURCHASE OR OBLIGATION NECESSARY TO ENTER

To enter, follow the directions published. **ALTERNATE MEANS OF ENTRY:** Hand-print your name and address on a 3"×5" card and mail to either: Silhouette Big Win, 3010 Walden Ave., P.O. Box 1867, Buffalo, NY 14269-1867, or Silhouette Big Win, P.O. Box 609, Fort Erie, Ontario L2A 5X3, and we will assign your Sweepstakes numbers (Limit: one entry per envelope). For eligibility, entries must be received no later than March 31, 1994 and be sent via 1st-class mail. No liability is assumed for printing errors or lost, late or misdirected entries.

To determine winners, the sweepstakes numbers on submitted entries will be compared against a list of randomly preselected prizewinning numbers. In the event all prizes are not claimed via the return of prizewinning numbers, random drawings will be held from among all other entries received to award unclaimed prizes.

Prizewinners will be determined no later than May 30, 1994. Selection of winning numbers and random drawings are under the supervision of D.L. Blair, Inc., an independent judging organization whose decisions are final. One prize to a family or organization. No substitution will be made for any prize, except as offered. Taxes and duties on all prizes are the sole responsibility of winners. Winners will be notified by mail. Chances of winning are determined by the number of entries distributed and received.

Sweepstakes open to persons 18 years of age or older, except employees and immediate family members of Torstar Corporation, D.L. Blair, Inc., their affiliates, subsidiaries and all other agencies, entities and persons connected with the use, marketing or conduct of this Sweepstakes. All applicable laws and regulations apply. Sweepstakes offer void wherever prohibited by law. Any litigation within the province of Quebec respecting the conduct and awarding of a prize in this Sweepstakes must be submitted to the Régies des Loteries et Courses du Quebec. In order to win a prize, residents of Canada will be required to correctly answer a time-limited arithmetical skill-testing question. Values of all prizes are in U.S. currency.

Winners of major prizes will be obligated to sign and return an affidavit of eligibility and release of liability within 30 days of notification. In the event of non-compliance within this time period, prize may be awarded to an alternate winner. Any prize or prize notification returned as undeliverable will result in the awarding of the prize to an alternate winner. By acceptance of their prize, winners consent to use of their names, photographs or other likenesses for purposes of advertising, trade and promotion on behalf of Torstar Corporation without further compensation, unless prohibited by law.

This Sweepstakes is presented by Torstar Corporation, its subsidiaries and affiliates in conjunction with book, merchandise and/or product offerings. Prizes are as follows: Grand Prize—$1,000,000 (payable at $33,333.33 a year for 30 years). First through Sixth Prizes may be presented in different creative executions, each with the following approximate values: First Prize—$35,000; Second Prize—$10,000; 2 Third Prizes—$5,000 each; 5 Fourth Prizes—$1,000 each; 10 Fifth Prizes—$250 each; 1,000 Sixth Prizes—$100 each. Prizewinners will have the opportunity of selecting any prize offered for that level. A travel-prize option if offered and selected by winner, must be completed within 12 months of selection and is subject to hotel and flight accommodations availability. Torstar Corporation may present this sweepstakes utilizing names other than Million Dollar Sweepstakes. For a current list of all prize options offered within prize levels and all names the Sweepstakes may utilize, send a self-addressed stamped envelope (WA residents need not affix return postage) to: Million Dollar Sweepstakes Prize Options/Names, P.O. Box 7410, Blair, NE 68009.

For a list of prizewinners (available after July 31, 1994) send a separate, stamped self-addressed envelope to: Million Dollar Sweepstakes Winners, P.O. Box 4728, Blair NE 68009.

SWPS693

WHERE WERE YOU WHEN THE LIGHTS WENT OUT?

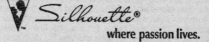

mp *good*

Relive the romance...
Harlequin and Silhouette
are proud to present

by Request™

A program of collections of three complete novels by the most requested authors with the most requested themes. Be sure to look for one volume each month with three complete novels by top name authors.

In June: **NINE MONTHS** Penny Jordan
Stella Cameron
Janice Kaiser

Three women pregnant and alone. But a lot can happen in nine months!

In July: **DADDY'S HOME** Kristin James
Naomi Horton
Mary Lynn Baxter

Daddy's Home... and his presence is long overdue!

In August: **FORGOTTEN PAST** Barbara Kaye
Pamela Browning
Nancy Martin

Do you dare to create a future if you've forgotten the past?

Available at your favorite retail outlet.

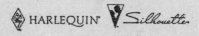